STRENGTH IN NUMBERS

KEITH MCNAIR

ISBN: 978-1-963068-33-7 (sc)
ISBN: 978-1-963068-34-4 (e)
ISBN: 978-1-963068-54-2 (hc)

Library of Congress Control Number: 2024904857

Previous novels by Keith McNair include

Split Decision
Fragmented Truths
Dancing in the Light
Dust to Dust
Carbon Residue

The strength of human touch is the power I have found in you. Allowing me to lean on you your kindness was given free and true.

Like a sister or a brother you were always there. Carrying me when I needed you and always showing that you cared.

Words of strength and honor are often spoken but rarely ever kept. Yet your unselfishness and compassion so much to me it has meant.

The strength of the human touch is a feeling bold and true. I've made it through a difficult time in life in no small part because of you.

k/mcnair

Victoria Reynolds examined the reflection in the full-length mirror that hung on the back of her bedroom door. A smile appeared across her face at the reflection that looked back at her.

Victoria wasn't self-righteous, but she appreciated the fact that she was an attractive thirty-two-year-old black woman that had attained so much success in life. Victoria managed to keep it all together well past her daughter Jasmine's growing pains. Victoria had to admit that she *"Had it going on,"* when it came to managing her home life and her career. However, there was that thing called romance and for the past several months Victoria felt its absence more than usual.

Since Raymond passed away more than three years ago Victoria had gone on a total of three dates. Victoria convinced herself that falling in love again was out of the question. Life now was all about family and career.

Irrefutably in that order.

Jasmine was seven-years old and when she was not with her grandparents, she occupied most of Victoria's free time. Jasmine was bright, energetic and a joy to have around. Although Victoria spent several days a month out of town on business, thoughts of Jasmine were never far away.

While Victoria did not consider herself as the world's perfect mother, she did the best job as humanly possible. Between the demands of being a working mother and having a career, for what it was worth Victoria saw herself as a survivor.

During her college years and prior to her marriage to Raymond, Victoria found it difficult to choose a single career path. She equally loved advertising and interior design. Victoria prepared herself for both. However, Raymond said that was a mistake. He said that success was about making a choice, sticking with that decision and then giving it everything you had. Doing anything less he said was complete disservice to yourself and your ambitions in life.

Although Victoria knew that Raymond meant no harm, there was something about the words he chose that bothered her. His choice caused Victoria to think of the assessment as a personal attack. However, in the end, Victoria realized that there was a significant amount of truth in the message. She also understood that at times there was a cost to be paid for the truth, and sometimes the truth can hurt.

Victoria mentally revisited Raymond's life journey as he once told her. Raymond understood how difficult it was for minorities to make it to the top of any profession. He said it was not always about realizing financial success. It was primarily about gaining respect from those above and below you in the workforce.

Raymond revealed that it took him years before he became a partner. The law firm of Jensen and McDale never had a person of color attain that position. Since becoming a partner, Raymond made it his mission to bring along as many ambitious litigators of color that he could find, be they male or female. From a business standpoint, Raymond was among the leaders in the firm when it came to increasing their bottom line. Raymond was successful in litigating his fair share of high-profiled cases which had not gone unnoticed and undoubtedly had something to do with his rise to the top.

However, and without warning fate dealt Raymond a tragic blow. Raymond passed away from cancer in the prime of his life. Sadly, his pancreatic cancer had gotten to the point where the disease spread to other organs and compromised their ability to function properly. Raymond was both a loving father and a son to his parents, but he poured everything into his work and his health suffered as a result. Victoria had also undergone an unexpected crisis in life. It was a change that she was not necessarily prepared for, yet with the support of family she just might make it. However, going forward she would have to do so without the love of her life.

A radio in the background called out the time. Victoria was running fifteen minutes off schedule. Her time spent with thoughts of the past had to end and bring her back to the present.

Victoria opened the door to her bedroom and called out to her daughter. Jasmine could hear her mother's voice yet that did not necessarily cause her to grease the wheels of motion. On most mornings Jasmine required physical stimulation to get her body moving. Today was no different. She groaned and pulled a pillow over her head as if to shut out the world.

It was a cold February morning and the temperature was not expected to rise above thirty-five degrees. Jasmine wanted to stay home but Mrs. Trent had scheduled a vocabulary test. In her opinion that was not the best way to begin the week.

"Come on Jasmine," Victoria called out once again.

"You have to get up now if you want a ride to school," Victoria added.

Victoria made a mental list of the things she had to accomplish. Prepare breakfast, make lunch for Jasmine, drop her off to school and get to the office in time for this morning's meeting. Cloning herself was a solution Victoria humorously thought.

"Let's go Jasmine," Victoria called out for a third time.

Jasmine usually made a big deal when her mother offered to take her to school. However today she had very little drive to call upon and it showed in her less than energetic movements.

A few moments later the smell of French toast filled the air. Jasmine's feet hit the floor and she moved as if hypnotized by the intoxicating aroma emanating from below.

"Do I have to take the bus home today or can grandma and grandpa pick me up?" Jasmine asked as if taking the bus were a punishment.

"Let's get out of the house first okay?" Victoria quickly responded.

"Besides we have to find out if grandma and grandpa have anything they need to do today," Victoria said.

"I hope not," Jasmine offered in a small and muffled tone.

"I heard that," Victoria said.

Victoria arrived at Real Time Advertising Agency just after nine o'clock. As the elevator car ascended toward twentieth floor Victoria mentally prepared herself for the morning. There was an executive meeting scheduled for ten o'clock. The agenda concerned a potential client that needed a slight nudge in the right direction.

The only serious competition was Eastwick and Dunham. However, it had been two years since they signed a new client. Real Time on the other hand recently signed Basden Technologies out of Boulder, Colorado. Notwithstanding the fact that it took two roundtrip flights out west and several tele-conference calls to seal the deal.

It should be a no brainer concerning their latest potential client Downing Sportswear. They were looking to move their advertising efforts in a new direction. To that point Victoria and her team had to present an effective dog and pony show. Perhaps one for the ages.

All cards in, this was big business. Success and delivery went hand in hand. Never over promise and under deliver Victoria believed.

The last quarter Real Time netted just under twenty million dollars in revenue. The fact that Victoria and her team had a direct hand in making that happen served to boost her confidence.

Along with their other products, Downing Sportswear designed athletic apparel for mature women. According to their prospectus the target audience were the forty-year and older age group. Their executives believed that mature women were under represented due to the focus on the so-called *"Generation-Z"* set.

While mature women had family responsibilities to contend with, they also had health concerns. Just as important to these women were being physically fit and looking the part. From what Victoria could imagine this was not something they were ready to give up. Being smart and sexy were all a part of the image they wanted to project. Victoria's thoughts turned to her mother. A real go-getter if ever there was one. She could see her mother checking off each descriptive box.

Throwing on a pair of baggy sweatpants and an over-sized tee-shirt was not the look mature women wanted. That was a look born from convenience and nothing more. Mature women want to go out in the world and be noticed. Staying home instead of joining a gym should not be considered off limits due to a lack of fashion. If there were a look they could call their own that would change everything. It was all about looking good and feeling the same way.

Victoria spent the next two weeks speaking with women in Downing Sportswear's target arena. She covered everything. From what they felt comfortable wearing to what outfit complemented their physic. From top to bottom and from lips to hips.

Victoria found that mature woman wanted to make an impact not only with their mind but with their look. This was the standard response across the board. As far as these women were concerned life was not about babysitting and baking cookies for their grandchildren. They had every right to feel alive and sexy. Although the medical industry offered a wide variety of solutions, many felt this was only a temporary fix. Not to mention the financial cost for physical beautification. These points struck a personal chord with Victoria. Years ago, she had a friend who had work done on her body to satisfy her partner and paid the ultimate price. Her family never understood the obsession nor could they get over the loss.

The representatives of Downing Sportswear were scheduled to arrive at eleven o'clock. Victoria had her game face on and was ready to hit the ground running. The power point presentation that her team put together covered all basis. Nothing was left to chance.

The meeting started on time where a number of ideas were presented to meet Dowling Sportswear's objectives. In attendance were their Chief Executive and Financial Officers. Victoria's team consisted of Brian Brentwood, Tracy McGinty and Victoria's right-hand Katherine Worthington.

Three hours later which included a thirty-minute lunch break, Real Time acquired a new client. The next steps boiled down to putting their plan of action into reality. There were some give and take on both sides of the table but it was nothing that would result in a deal breaker.

After all was said and done everyone walked away with a sense of accomplishment.

Victoria had just exited the lobby of her office building when her cell phone rang.

"Vicky, its mom. I was hoping to catch you before you left the office. How's my timing?" Gayle asked.

Victoria instantly recalled how mom had referred to her as Vicky every now and then for as long as she could remember.

"About ten minutes south of lousy," Victoria responded in a humorous manner.

"I guess you can't have everything in life. I called to remind you to pick up dessert for dinner tonight," Gayle said.

Victoria remained silent which said everything.

"It sounds like someone forgot," Gayle said. "But that's all right. At least you won't have to worry about baking a cake. Just pick up something from the bakery and all will be forgiven," Gayle promised.

"I'm sorry mom. I'm not sure if it's a matter of me juggling too much or something worse," Victoria offered.

"In my case it's a little bit of both at times, especially when you get to my age," Gayle said taking a small shot at herself.

"Not likely mom. Your mind is as sharp as anyone I know, Victoria said."

"True. But I wish you would remind your father of that fact. You would think that after more than thirty-years of marriage a wife's law would be absolute."

"Don't worry about dad. I'll talk to him tonight and if he doesn't come around, I know his weakness," Victoria said with a tone of confidence.

In unison each woman spoke the same words. "Homemade cherry pie."

Victoria surprised Jasmine telling her that she would be coming along with her to San Francisco. Victoria watched the look of joy appear on Jasmine's face as she took in the news.

"It's only for a few days," Victoria said.

"That's great mom," Jasmine replied with unbridled enthusiasm.

"When do we leave? Should I start picking out my outfits now?" Jasmine asked.

"Hold on just a minute honey," Victoria began.

"We leave on Thursday. Which according to the calendar is three days away. So save some of that energy for the trip," Victoria said.

During the second day of the trip Jasmine spoke about everything that was happening in school. The good as well as the bad. Jasmine spoke about her plans for the future and how she wanted to be just like her mother.

From there Jasmine opened up about her inner feelings. She revealed how losing her dad affected the way she behaved in school and at home. Victoria recalled that period in Jasmine's life. She understood everything that Jasmine was going through. Victoria felt Jasmine's ups, downs and the rollercoaster ride of emotions that plagued her. When Raymond passed away Jasmine became withdrawn. She seemed to have had no interest in the things she and her dad used to do.

Victoria tried to break down the walls Jasmine built around herself. Yet she failed at every turn. Victoria began to worry that Jasmine would never be the same. She feared that Jasmine would close herself off from everyone she knew. However, as time passed Victoria once again saw the light of life shine in Jasmine's eyes and in her personality. Whatever caused the reversal Victoria was not going to question. She was simply grateful that it happened.

Jasmine was their miracle child. Victoria had miscarried twice before their prayers were answered. Victoria was told that her uterus was too weak to allow a fetus to fully develop. More importantly, a third miscarriage could put her life in jeopardy. Concerned about Victoria's health Raymond suggested that they consider adoption. Victoria was quick to voice her opposition.

Although she was not an overtly religious person Victoria chose to put things in God's hands. She believed that He would make their dream come true. Raymond and Victoria's prayers were eventually answered when Victoria announced that she was pregnant. Raymond found out later that Victoria had been monitoring her body through pregnancy tests. On one level Raymond was upset that Victoria chose to keep him in the dark. Yet he was sympathetic enough to understand and respect her for what she had done. Victoria explained that this was not easy and she had considered Raymond's feelings. Raymond had done everything to keep her spirits high. But this was something Victoria believed she had to do. If Raymond loved her then he would understand Victoria convinced herself.

Upon hearing the news about the pregnancy. Victoria's parents as well as Raymond's family showered them with their blessings. They thanked God that the couple's prayers had been answered. Raymond was not sure about an all-powerful supreme being. However, he had to admit that divine intervention was a distinct possibility.

In the months that followed Victoria told her mother that Raymond made a nuisance of himself. Although she loved every minute of it, Victoria confessed that she was going to need a vacation to some tropical desert island.

Victoria and Jasmine took time to shop and take in the sights that San Francisco had to offer. However, the vacation had to end at some point.

The last two days were spent doing "girly-girl" things as Jasmine put it. Victoria would buy something for Jasmine then the roles were reversed. In spite of her age Jasmine had a great eye for fashion. Victoria guessed that when the time came Jasmine was going to give some poor guy more than he could handle.

During dinner Jasmine excitedly spoke about the gifts for her grandparents. Suddenly Jasmine posed a question that she must have been struggling with judging by the expression on her face.

"Mom, do you ever think about getting married again?" Jasmine asked with the innocence of youth shielding her from her mother's possible anger.

The question took Victoria completely by surprise. Jasmine's inquiry was not what she expected when she considered the day they just had. Victoria could feel a tightness form in her chest as if a 500-pound gorilla sat there. This was another one of those times where Victoria had to be truthful with Jasmine. This was about how life worked.

Her life in particular.

"What would make you ask something like that?" Victoria asked.

"In school last week some of the kids were talking about being raised by a single parent. A boy named Kenny lives with his mother because his mom and dad got divorced. Someone brought it up to Mrs. Trent and she explained it to the whole class."

"What did Mrs. Trent say about divorce?" Victoria asked.

"Mrs. Trent said that divorce happens when two people have differences they can't work through. Is that true mom. Don't they love each other anymore?" Jasmine asked with a tone of confusion in her voice.

"Were those Mrs. Trent's exact words?" Victoria asked.

"Well maybe not exactly those words," Jasmine responded.

A thoughtful expression creased Victoria's face. She didn't want to give Jasmine the wrong impression on the subject. Children were like sponges. They would absorb comments made by their parents on most occasions. Sadly, there are times when those words were released at an inappropriate time.

Victoria adjusted her position and placed her right hand on Jasmine's left before responding.

"When two people divorce it doesn't necessarily mean that they don't love each other anymore. There could be a thousand reasons why it happens," Victoria offered.

"Mom did you and daddy ever talk about divorce when he got sick?" Jasmine's eyes became soft and slightly moist as she waited for a response.

Victoria wanted to dive under the table and avoid giving a response. The subject was difficult enough to discuss between adult to adult. But Victoria remembered that her parents were always upfront with her. Especially mom. Although dad was there when she needed him, it was mom who would explain certain things. Especially things when it came to growing up as a member of the opposite sex. Mom explained that when she was growing up there were things that were not discussed in the house. She said that was the way things worked back then. However, the world had changed so much since then. Kids today were able to teach adults more than they cared to know in some situations. It was a reality that Victoria did not always feel comfortable having to face.

Victoria snapped back to the present.

"To answer your question. No daddy and I never thought about or talked about divorce and neither did your grandparents," Victoria said with a sense of pride.

Jasmine was not finished.

"What about when you and daddy argued?" Jasmine asked.

"Yes, Jasmine dad and I argued sometimes, but it was nothing that would lead to a divorce. We loved each other too much for that to happen. But more importantly, we loved you."

Jasmine's question seemed genuine and troubling at the same time and Victoria had some difficulty in holding back a smile.

Victoria took a moment to take in the expression on Jasmine's face. There was another question at the ready wrapped in a smile. But Victoria continued before Jasmine could speak.

"The weird thing about arguments is making up and then not remembering what caused the argument in the first place. Your grandmother told me that married people should never go to bed angry. She said that husbands and wives should resolve any problems before the next morning because they never knew what the night may bring."

Victoria was pretty sure that Jasmine understood her grandmother's words and seemed to be satisfied since there were no other questions on the subject.

Jasmine's face brightened when the waiter brought over the dessert menu. It was as if the previous conversation had never occurred.

This was the third time Wesley had to relieve himself. It was one-thirty in the morning. He and Gayle had gone to bed relatively early at nine o'clock. Gayle was in a deep sleep and nothing short of wild horses galloping across the roof could disturb her. That being the case it was easy enough to slip out of bed undetected.

Wesley stood in front of the toilet bowl waiting for his stream to begin. He could feel the cold tiled floor against the bottom of his feet. In response his body released an involuntary shiver. Gayle had always fussed with him about putting on his slippers if he got up during the night. Wesley felt that he was getting way with something and as a result he accepted this small victory.

Wesley waited another few seconds. Then finally relief came as his liquid began to flow. However, much to his disappointment only a few drops hit the water. He was disappointed that the false alarm pulled him from such a restful state. The way he felt moments ago, Wesley thought he would be standing in front of the bowl for at least five minutes and able to extinguish a small fire.

Wesley washed his hands and returned to bed hoping he could get back to sleep.

Hours later the aroma of breakfast pulled Wesley into consciousness. His favorite meal of the day. Coffee, bacon, eggs and cinnamon toast. Wesley was known to have consumed a similar plate of food well beyond the daylight hours of the morning.

The bedroom was bathed in sunlight. Gayle must have opened the curtains and blinds before she left. Wesley sat on the edge of the bed with the palms of his hands resting on both knees. His back was slightly arched forward. He was feeling pretty good and looking forward to a productive day. However, when he rose to his feet a stabbing pain raced through his lower back with the force of a sledge hammer. Wesley let out a loud groan as the pain increased when he took a step forward. Wesley held his breath in fear of being struck once again. He slowly let out his breath as if he were extinguishing a candle on a birthday cake.

After a minute Wesley noticed that the pain had eased in its intensity and mercifully, he was able to move around with no further discomfort. Wesley figured it must have been a muscle spasm. He had been working in the backyard and the strain on his body must have caught up with him. Simple as that.

Wesley chose not to mention anything to Gayle simply because she would in his opinion make matters worse with her constant *'should haves and should not haves.'*

Wesley decided that he would take a few pain killers after breakfast and before he began his errands for the day. He had to drop a few letters and packages at the post office, Gayle wanted to go to the fabric store and he wanted to rent a few movies for tonight. No problem he thought. Piece of cake.

The next sound he heard was Gayle.

"Let's go Wes. Shake a leg up there. Breakfast is on the table," Gayle called out from the kitchen.

"And good morning back to you," Wesley responded, knowing that Gayle was not able to hear him. His response was simply a matter of reflex that he couldn't pull back.

Although Victoria was ecstatic about the time away with Jasmine, she was glad to be back home. Now it was all about business. Implementing the plan of action that was discussed a few weeks ago ruled her thoughts. The days and weeks to come would without a doubt challenge her ability to perform under extreme pressure.

Victoria was more than ready to get started.

Soon after Victoria ended what she hoped was the last call of the day with Katherine her phone rang. A groan of disapproval escaped from within.

It was Sharon Ramsey. There was an immediate reversal in sentiment. Sharon had been with the Finance Department for more than ten years and Victoria always thought of her as a mentor. She was one of the first people to explain how the corporate world worked. She said that being unprepared could tear you to pieces and spit you out without remorse. Sharon didn't bullshit when it came to their business or the politics it produced. There were times when Sharon's bluntness ruffled more than a few feathers. But with Sharon you accepted the good and the bad under the same umbrella. The rumor was that if you royally fucked up with Sharon there would be hell to pay. She was not one to easily forgive and forget.

One of Sharon's favorite sayings went like this, "The good Lord is in the business of forgiving. Me, I'm just a simple human being so don't expect too much."

Victoria understood early on in their friendship that hearts and flowers were not Sharon's thing.

At five-thirty Victoria, Sharon, Rachel Thompson and Carole Jenkins met in the lobby. At Rachel's suggestion they agreed to go to The Papier Mache. It was a new restaurant which opened on Madison Avenue and Fifty-Third Street just over a month ago.

Rachel being the artist of the group fell in love with the restaurant because of its name. On any given night you might find clientele from the political arena, the world of fashion and Hollywood all in attendance. They all wanted to see and be seen in the same breath.

The cuisine according to the article Rachel read was to die for, reincarnate yourself and enjoy once again. They featured one of the finest arrays of wines imported from around the world. Their executive chef Andre Sinclair recently came aboard after attaining a major following in Paris.

Once the quartet entered the restaurant they were immediately blown away by the layout. The article did little justice in its description of the interior. Each of the women had been to impressive restaurants before but The Papier Mache was head and shoulders above anything they had previously experienced. Victoria offered to buy Rachel her first drink as a reward based on her recommendation.

As a complimentary gift all women dining tonight were presented with a long-stemmed red rose.

The party was led to their table by a tall red-haired gentlemen. He was dressed in a suit which resembled a tuxedo. In an English accent he introduced himself as Brent. He handed menus to each of the women and stated that he would be back for their drink orders.

Carole admitted to being in love with the sound of his voice once he was out of earshot.

"If you play your cards right, I'll find out if he's available," Sharon offered.

"With my luck he's probably gay and seeing one of the cooks in the kitchen," Carole responded. "But you're more than willing to give it a try. I can't remember the last time I did the horizontal salsa with the opposite sex."

Victoria thoughts briefly turned to her station and what could be done to better her life in the same area that Carole just mentioned. Interestingly enough, it had nothing to do with dancing. The conversation turned away from work and switched to more important things in life. Family.

Sharon revealed that when she needed some space her husband took over with the kids. This gave her a chance to unwind and put any negative energy from the working day aside.

Rachel saw this as an opportunity to play the devil's advocate. Rachel was always a troublemaker as a child. She never let an opportunity to pour salt into an open wound pass her by.

"When does he get to take off the apron and kick up his heels and is he a good little boy about it?" Rachel asked in a sarcastic manner.

Everyone at the table believed that Sharon was going to lay into Rachel for what they saw as her crossing the line.

However, that wasn't the case. Sharon responded with as much grace as Victoria had ever witnessed under the circumstances.

"Let me put it to you this way," Sharon began. "My cat never strays far away from home and he loves the way I scratch his back at night. Any more questions?" Sharon emphatically asked.

Victoria and Carole lifted their glasses in Sharon's direction at her ability to put Rachel in her place with elegant efficiency.

The remainder of the evening went by without any further verbal attacks from Rachel. The quartet focused on movies, books, and potential vacation destinations. Then the subject of relationships came around. There was a long discussion about the differences between enjoying sex and being in love and having sex. However, it was Carole's version of the two positions that took everyone by surprise. She believed that having sex and being in love were on opposite sides of the same coin. Carole had no qualms about expressing that while sex was an important part of any relationship, it shouldn't be the basis for getting involved in one.

"But where does love fit into your equation?" Victoria asked. The tone of her voice was not meant to challenge Carole's opinion. It was simply an attempt to understand her line of thinking on the subject of sex. It was also her way of gaining some insight into Carole's life outside of work.

"Love?" Carol asked with a puzzled look on her face. "Love is something that occupies a space on its own. Haven't you figured that out yet? Having a sexual encounter or three without any attachments is not necessarily a bad thing. As long as it's understood that things may or may not go any further." Carole said with a sense of conviction.

"Okay," Rachel began. "That may be your prospective, but what about the guy's feelings? You know how some men react when it comes to sex," Rachel chimed in.

"A lasting sexual relationship is not something to be taken lightly. Also, when does the issue of respect come into play?" Rachel continued.

Sharon sat back with her drink in hand. She watched the exchange between the women waiting for the right moment to add her thoughts into the mix.

Carole inhaled and exhaled loudly before responding. She was upset with herself for bringing up her sexual preferences in the first place. It was not her intention to have to defend her lifestyle among the people she considered friends. But it was too late for any regrets.

"Listen, we're all grown and successful women with the ability to make intelligent choices. Relationships with the opposite sex or the same sex for that matter play a role in our daily lives. This is a fact no matter how we might try and avoid the potential collision. I simply try to make the best of the situation and avoid any conflicts or pit falls," Carole said.

There was an awkward momentarily silence. Victoria and Rachel looked down at their drinks as if counting the floating ice cubes in their respective glasses.

Carol continued speaking.

"Now, about that level of respect you mentioned," Carol said directing her response at Rachel as if the other members of their party were invisible.

"At times it has to be reinforced. But it's definitely there. Respect should never be swept under the rug for the sake of a sexual tryst. So you see Rachel, my life as it stands couldn't be any better."

Victoria, Rachel and Sharon realized that Carol was being true to her convictions. This was the way she chose to live. Unchanging and unrepentant. Each woman secretly wondered if there were a part of Carol lurking inside of them waiting to be acknowledged and released. Unchanging and unrepentant.

Just before they went their separate ways the quartet promised that they'd meet for dinner next week. Carol volunteered to choose the restaurant.

It was just after two-o'clock on a Wednesday afternoon and Victoria finally found a moment to herself. The morning had been filled with meetings and telephone calls to be made and returned. Up until this point Victoria seemed to have been pushed and pulled in a thousand different directions. Everyone wanted something from her with the belief that their needs were more important than the preceding individual. As a result, it made for a frustrating morning. Not to mention the physical toll it took on her.

Victoria could feel the pounding in her temples rise. Popping a few extra strength tablets would be a waste of time and effort. Victoria was proud of her success but on days like today blue skies and sandy beaches called out her name.

Victoria leaned back in her chair and stared at the ceiling above. She absently counted the square tiles above while rummaging through the corridors of her mind. Mom picked up Jasmine from school which allowed Victoria time to treat herself. She decided to leave the office much earlier than usual.

Forty-five minutes later Victoria found herself at Evelyn's Boutique. There was a leather handbag that she spotted last week and had to have.

Victoria wasn't sure exactly what it was, but something pulled at her after leaving the boutique. Suddenly there was no rush to go home. Victoria thought about a devil sitting on one shoulder and an angel sitting on the other. Each spewed advice on how she should spend the next few hours.

And the winner is…

Victoria wasn't much of a drinker by any stretch. However, she would have one to celebrate her short-lived freedom. The time away gave her a chance to think about a variety of subjects. Victoria understood that if love were to come around again it would not be a bad thing. But the challenge she faced was in where to begin.

Uncertainties in life were as consistent as the rising sun. Victoria recalled someone telling her that finding love and happiness was like riding a bicycle. You never forget how to enjoy either one. Especially if you're lucky enough for true love to find you even once in a lifetime. But a second time around was next to impossible. Victoria appreciated the possibility, but she was too much of a cynic to appreciate their meaning or live through the potential reality.

At his age Wesley expected to experience some sleepless nights. But as he sat in Dr. McCain's office filling out the medical questionnaire, he could barely focus on the papers in front of him. Wesley made every effort trying to hide this from Gayle.

Over the past several days Wesley had no energy to do much of anything around the house. Keeping his lack of drive from Gayle had become increasingly difficult day after day. On more than one occasion she blamed him for not taking care of himself. She was that constant voice of reason who keep reminding him that keeping his doctor appointments were important. Wesley realized that his wife's nagging and constant monitoring was a matter of her concern for his overall well-being and nothing more. But at times he felt as if she were treating him like a child or a doting old fool.

"Remember to sign the bottom of the page," Gayle reminded Wesley as if he had never filled out important documents before.

"Also, when the doctor asks how you have been feeling tell him everything. It's important that you don't leave anything out. Understand?" Gayle urged.

Wesley clenched his jaw tightly almost to the point of shattering his teeth. This was the only way he could relieve the tension that was building up inside as a result of his wife's uninvited "advice."

"My God woman," Wesley began. "You'd think I've never done something like this before. Believe it or not I can still walk and chew gum at the same time. So I don't think I'll have much difficulty with reading and understanding a simple form." There was a tone of annoyance in his voice that he could not hide. However, Wesley would never openly admit it but he was anxious as hell. Wesley realized weeks before that something was not quite right with him considering the way he had been feeling. The cold he had several weeks ago hung around much longer than he or Gayle expected. It seemed that he failed to bounce back as quickly as he had done in the past. Granted he was not a young spring rooster that could get up at the crack of dawn any longer. But he never expected the physical problems that he had been going through lately. Maybe he was getting old after all Wesley silently teased himself.

Under Gayle's watchful eyes Wesley scanned the documents he completed for accuracy and completeness. As her husband checked over the forms Gayle took the opportunity to look around the room. She counted the number of patients that had arrived earlier.

Seven.

Gayle wished that Wesley had the forethought to schedule his appointment much earlier. She had things to take care of and sitting around in the doctor's office wasn't high on her list. But that wasn't something that she would bring up to Wesley because he'd probably accuse her of nagging him. But everyone under the sun knew it was his fault for their being late. Gayle loved Wesley with all of her heart, but sometimes that man . . .

Gayle sat and watched as the nurse took Wesley's vitals. Blood pressure, height, weight and breathing. She ended the examination by drawing two vials of his blood. The nurse was not very talkative as she went about her duties. When she did speak her voice was almost mechanical and there was very little warmth about her.

"Dr. McCain will be with you shortly," she said before leaving.

After ten minutes had passed Dr. McCain appeared. He stood a full six feet-three inches tall and appeared to spend as much time in the gym as he did on his practice. Dr. McCain was an imposing man from a physical stand point, yet he was one of the most caring and gentle individuals that Wesley and Gayle had ever known. In many respects he reminded Gayle of her younger brother Brian right down to the hint of freckles around his nose and cheeks.

"So Wesley it's been quite a while hasn't it?" Dr. McCain opened as he held Wesley's medical chart in his hand.

With guilt clearly written across his face Wesley slightly turned away and cleared his throat.

"I've been busy working around the house that's all. You know how it is when you own a home. There's always something that needs to be fixed, painted or replaced," Wesley offered in his defense.

"But not where your health is concerned," Gayle interjected. The doctor gave Gayle a look of approval.

Wesley not so much.

"I can understand that. But no one will ever blame you for sitting still and leaving things to be done by a professional every once in a while. You have to think about your health," Dr. McCain calmly said.

"All right," Wesley replied in resignation.

"How have you been feeling since your last physical?" the doctor asked.

In the back of his mind Wesley replayed Gayle's words about being straight forward and truthful when asked about his health.

"Sometimes I have trouble sleeping through the night, Wesley confessed."

Wesley's words were barely audible. He felt a bit uneasy speaking in front of Gayle. This in spite of the fact that he spent a good portion of his adult life with her. Talking about his shortcomings still bothered him. Perhaps it was something he got from his father who was a proud man that never discussed his health issues when they arose. Wesley conceded that this was a character flaw hard-wired into his personality.

Wesley cleared his throat again before he began.

"Sometimes I have to go more than three times at night. But it doesn't happen often," Wesley added quickly as if to take away some concern that appeared on the doctor's face.

"How many times a week would you say this occurs?" the doctor asked.

"About two, maybe three times a week," Wesley responded.

"Okay. On those nights at what time did you have your last meal including any liquids?" Dr. McCain asked while making notes in Wesley's file.

Wesley was silent while mentally recalling the past week. There was that late night snack on Wednesday, consisting of roast beef on rye and two glasses of lemonade. The following night—Wesley didn't want to think about.

"I ate something late twice last week," Wesley confessed. "Nothing major though," he added sheepishly.

"First thing. You're going to have to stop eating anything past your last meal of the day. Furthermore, you should have that last meal between six-thirty and eight o'clock at night on any day of the week. That way if you retire by nine, nine-thirty you will have the opportunity to clear your bowels."

Gayle gave herself a pat on the back realizing that this was the very same advice she had been preaching for weeks.

But sometimes good advice fell on deaf ears when it came to Wesley.

Dr. McCain turned his attention away from Wesley before speaking.

"Gayle I know it might be difficult, but you're going to have to keep him on the straight and narrow path. His good health just might depend on it." The doctor's voice was warm and spoke with a sense of confidence that his advice would be taken to heart.

Gayle nodded in response to the instructions.

Dr. McCain turned back to Wesley.

"Remember two years when your cholesterol was at 9.7 and with a regiment of proper dieting and exercise we managed to get that number down? Well, you're going to have to get back to that lifestyle and stick with it," Dr. McCain said.

"Although not necessarily related as a major cause, continued high blood sugar levels can and may result in arteries becoming blocked. While I don't have or am aware of the percentage of individuals where this may occur, I do want to make you aware of the possibility," the doctor added.

This was Wesley's chance to come clean regarding his health issues that were previously undisclosed. Without much stimulation Wesley revealed several other personal ailments that had plagued him over the past few weeks. The shortness in breath, the headaches and the difficulty he experienced at fully clearing his bowels.

Hearing himself speak Wesley could not help wonder why he waited so long to reveal this part of his history. But he knew the answer already. His father's personality toward secrecy may very well have become part of his own behavior.

Wesley understood that everything the doctor said was the truth. However, he did not want the words forced down his throat so to speak. Having Gayle nod in agreement at the doctor's words only made matters worse. Yet to a larger degree Wesley realized that if he wanted to continue on with his so-called golden years, something had to be done and a change in his habits was at the top of the list.

Although he was not as active as in years past, Wesley definitely subscribed to the adage that you were only as young as you feel. He understood that mental youth was just as important to a person's physical wellbeing.

"I'd like you to start by changing your diet over the next three months. After that time, we'll run your numbers again," Dr. McCain said.

The tone, body language and the expression on the doctor's face told Wesley that this was no time for excuses. Dr. McCain made some additional notes in the file before turning his attention back to Wesley.

"Here is some information I want both of you to review which should help with the transition to a healthier diet and exercise program. Wesley, I recommend that you start with something low impact and go from there. How does that sound?" the doctor asked.

Both Wesley and Gayle thanked the doctor for the information and promised that they would take his recommendations seriously.

After Wesley and Gayle left, Dr. McCain thought about plans toward Wesley's treatment. Wesley indicated that his stream was interrupted and at times he experienced a slight burning sensation upon urination. At Wesley's age and combined with his other symptoms this was not a good sign. There would be the usual blood and urine tests and he would throw in an updated sonogram for good measure. It was a good idea to get a look at Wesley's internal organs to see if there were any irregularities to be addressed.

In the past Wesley's test results resulted in his being given a clean bill of health. However, Dr. McCain realized that could change based on what he had just heard.

With that being said Dr. McCain's thoughts turned to his next patient—Sharon Holloway.

It was one restless night. Victoria managed a little more than four hours of peaceful sleep. Her body ached and no amount of pain medication she had consumed made her feel better. The only consolation being it was a Saturday and for the next two days she did not have to deal with anything related to work.

It was eight o'clock in the morning and Jasmine was still quiet. During the week it was almost impossible to get her going. On most weekends she was up at the crack of dawn with a motor running at full throttle. Weekends usually consisted of planning events for the next two days. The menu was different each time. They would spend time visiting her grandparents, a trip to Brooklyn and sometimes they would take the railroad to Long Island. The farms on the South Fork were always a favorite.

Just as Victoria completed her thought Jasmine burst into the room and jumped head first onto the unmade queen-sized bed.

"Hey mom do you know what I want to do today? We can . . ."

"Hold on young lady. Don't I deserve a good morning kiss or something?" Victoria asked in an attempt to stem her daughter's enthusiasm.

"Well . . ." Jasmine began as if the question were a matter open for debate.

Victoria rolled over and began feverishly tickling Jasmine's mid-section. The child's morning greeting was barely coherent due to her hysterical laughter.

"Now what was that you were about to ask?" Victoria offered once the action had slowed down a bit.

"I was talking with Anita and Brenda yesterday and I was wondering if . . ."

Jasmine stopped before completing her sentence. She was not sure if her mother would agree with the idea of having company over for the day. Weekends were usually their time.

"C'mon. Out with it," Victoria said after witnessing the look of hesitation on her daughter's face.

"I was wondering if Anita and Brenda can come over this afternoon and hang out for a while."

Victoria recalled a few weeks ago when Jasmine swore that she would never speak to Anita again. Apparently, they got into an argument at school over a test score. Supposedly that was the end of their longstanding friendship. It was a she said she said kind of thing. Jasmine was so angry with Anita that nothing could be said to change her mind or temper the rage brewing in her small frame.

But now she was asking if Anita could come over. The whole thing seemed incredibly weird for Victoria's logical and structured universe to comprehend.

When she was much younger, her mother said that girls are quicker to argue with one another and then make up in a short period of time. Victoria wondered if she ran as hot and cold as a child.

Her mother said that boys were different. They fought over silly things and never made time to say they were sorry. Victoria recalled hearing Jasmine refer to boys as jerks on more than one occasion. As a mother Victoria marveled at the tone of anger in the voice of one so young and unaccustomed to the workings of the world.

"Have you cleared things with their parents?" Victoria asked knowing full well that Jasmine had not.

"Well not exactly. We talked about it during school yesterday. But I'm sure if you called, their parents would say yes," Jasmine said hoping that a dose of charm would work on her mother.

Victoria remained silent taking in Jasmine's smiling face.

"You can use some of that magic you use at work," Jasmine said as she continued to push her case.

After the words left her mouth Jasmine was not sure if she had crossed the line between adult and childhood. Jasmine heard her mother on the phone saying that children were famous for testing the limits of their parent's patience. However, Jasmine never thought of herself as one of "those children," but at the same time she understood that she was no angel.

Victoria knew when someone was laying it on a little too thick, but that was something she never expected from Jasmine.

Spending time with Anita and Brenda was obviously important. This appeared to be true not only because of Jasmine's plea, but the look in her eyes said it all. Victoria could see that taking something this important away from her would be a mistake. There was something to be said about earning points with your child. The difference in age hardly mattered.

"All right. I'll call their parents after breakfast," Victoria said.

"To be honest mom I'm not that hungry," Jasmine said attempting to still the excitement churning inside of her body.

"Remember I had seconds last night, so . . ."

"Jasmine Michelle don't even go there. I'm willing to give in but there will be no skipping breakfast today or any other day," Victoria said.

"Ok. You're the best mom," Jasmine said as she clung to Victoria's neck.

Jasmine flew out of the bedroom in a blur and into the bathroom to begin washing up. Her next stop was the kitchen where she fixed herself a bowl of her favorite cold cereal.

At ten-fifteen Victoria called both parents who gave the okay to have their respective daughters spend the day with Jasmine.

After spending several hours at the mall Victoria wished she had not been such a pushover this morning. Three young girls who loved to browse and shop their lives away were more than she had expected. But at the same Victoria appreciated the bond of friendship the three girls displayed in spite of their earlier emotion of anger.

By five o'clock Anita and Brenda were picked up by their parents. Jasmine had disappeared and was more than likely in her room going through her "loot" purchased earlier in the day. Victoria imagined that Anita and Benda were doing the same thing.

Victoria sat at the kitchen counter with the mail in one hand and a glass of Chablis in the other. There was a large compliment of junk mail consisting of advertisements for home improvement services, vehicle purchases and discounts to be had from department stores in the area.

Mixed in with the unwanted pile of mail there was a card addressed to Jasmine from her grandfather. Victoria was surprised to see the words happy birthday written across the back of the envelope. However, Jasmine's birthday was at least two weeks away.

Victoria looked at the bright pink envelope this time focusing on the return address. She noticed that it did not have the peel and place sticker that her mother used when mailing a letter. This one was handwritten by her father. Victoria opened the envelope and found a birthday card with Jasmine's name on it and a crisp twenty-dollar bill inside. There was also a note by dad expressing his regrets for missing Jasmine's birthday. This was the second time in as many weeks that dad did something well . . . strange was the best way Victoria could put it. Earlier this week dad spoke about the dinner they had as if it happened yesterday. In reality they had dinner more than a month ago. Victoria wondered if she should mention anything to mom about his behavior or leave it alone. Sometimes her memory was not the sharpest and the saying about people who lived in glass houses came to mind.

Last week she thought she had forwarded a report to the research division. However, she left the report in her office filed away with some other unrelated paperwork. Misplacing her keys was another thing on the list that seemed to always test her memory. Victoria realized that her own glass house needed protecting and she had better be careful before throwing any shade in her father's direction.

After dinner and Jasmine's bath Victoria was ready to call it an evening. She kissed Jasmine goodnight before making her way down the hall toward her bedroom.

Just as she plopped down on the mattress her phone came alive.

"Hey mom. How's it going?" Victoria began.

"I called earlier but I guess you were out," Gayle said sounding mildly disappointed.

"I'm sorry I missed your call. Jasmine and I were out with her friends for most of the day. So, what are you and dad up to this evening?" Victoria asked.

"Nothing much. The highlight of the day was spent at the nursery. We bought some shrubs for the backyard. Now the problem is getting your father to plant them before they die. He did the same thing last year. We bought some Azaleas to line the fence but your father got busy with other things so we had to call in a landscaper. Your father was pretty upset because he felt I went behind his back. But something had to be done. What do you think?" Gayle asked in conclusion.

Victoria was not sure how she should respond to her mother's question. It was rare when she took sides between her parents no matter what had previously occurred. Victoria believed that doing so would only cause more problems. Instead, she decided to change the subject.

"Mom, you know that I'm not much of a peace maker when it comes to you and dad, but why don't I come over and cook dinner tomorrow night?" Victoria offered.

It had been almost a full year since Victoria prepared a meal for her parents. Taking them out to dinner a couple times a month didn't count so Victoria felt this would be as much a treat for her as she hoped it would be for them.

"That sounds nice," Gayle simply responded. Ignoring the fact that Victoria blew off her question.

"I think your father would like that. Do you have anything special in mind?" Gayle asked.

"You know me mom. I can usually come up with something edible and I guarantee there will be no leftovers," Victoria said with emphasis.

"Do you need me to get anything from the supermarket for you?" Gayle asked.

"Not a thing. I've got it all under control," Victoria said brimming with confidence at her culinary skills.

Victoria and Jasmine arrived at her parent's house at four o'clock the following day. While Victoria focused her energy on preparing dinner, Jasmine spent time entertaining her grandparents showing off her video game skills.

Three hours later everyone had gathered in the living room for dessert. Victoria purchased a New York Cheesecake from Sergio's and a pound of fresh ground coffee. Jasmine worked her way through a bowl of strawberry ice cream drenched in a chocolate sauce.

Victoria was ecstatic that mom and dad loved her stuffed pork chops, wild rice and steamed broccoli. Victoria kept it a secret that she got the recipe from a co-worker. Although she added just enough of her own ingredients to claim a measure of originality.

"Not too bad of a cook it seems," Wesley added as he rubbed his mid-section.

"Careful with that cake," Gayle said as she shook her index finger in her husband's direction.

"You remember what Doctor McCain said," she added.

At hearing about dad's visit to the doctor, Victoria turned toward her mother, ready to ask questions.

"It was nothing serious," Wesley immediately chimed in as if reading the non-verbal look of concern on his daughter's face.

"I just went in for a checkup that's all. Having a second slice of cake will not put me at death's door you know." Wesley's comments were directed toward his wife.

Victoria took the moment of silence to change the subject knowing that she would get the full story from her mother at a later time. Victoria knew that her dad always kept his health issues close to the vest.

"Dad, have you heard anything from Aunt Janice since she moved?" Victoria asked.

In spite of the fact that Victoria was a grown woman with a family of her own she always respected her elders. There was never a time that Aunt Janice was known by any other title.

Gayle thought for a moment before turning Wesley.

"We spoke to her last week. It was last Thursday, right?"

"Janice. Who is that?" Wesley responded with a puzzled look on his face.

Gayle and Victoria looked at each other sure that Wesley was teasing them. Although they knew that brother and sister loved each other, they could be single minded and driven in their views as any republican and democrat can be. Their opposing views were legendary within the family and they sometimes fought tooth and nail if there were a political issue open for debate.

When they looked closely at Wesley and directly into his eyes each could tell that the question was genuine.

Victoria made an attempt to lighten up an otherwise tense moment.

"C'mon dad you remember Aunt Janice. How in the world could you forget someone like her?"

"Wesley are you okay?" There was an immediate tone of concern in Gayle's voice.

Wesley was silent. It seemed as if he didn't hear the question. There was no sense of recognition on his face and for the moment his mind seemed to tell him that he was in a room with strangers.

Wesley leaned back from his seated position. Both hands rested on his knees.

"I've got a strong urge for something sweet. Is any there dessert?" Wesley asked.

Victoria watched as her father spoke. It seemed he was not specifically addressing anyone in the room when he spoke.

Gayle placed her cup of coffee on the table and moved closer to her husband. She placed one hand on his shoulder and the other on top of his left hand.

"We just had dessert. Don't you remember, Victoria brought over a cheese cake?" Gayle said.

Without another word being spoken it appeared as if a cloud had been removed from Wesley's mind and he once again joined the present.

"Of course we just had dessert. I think I'm going to pay dearly for having that second slice of cake though," he confessed.

Wesley spoke as if his temporary bout of amnesia had not occurred. After taking in Wesley's comment, mother and daughter were stunned leaving them to wonder if they had actually witnessed what had happened.

The passing seconds seemed to hang in the air as if slowed by time itself. Victoria could read the look of concern on her mother's face and decided to do something to change the direction of the evening.

On slightly unsteady legs Victoria rose from the couch and approached her mother.

"Okay mom let's get this cake out of here before dad goes for a third slice," Victoria said in a humorous manner.

"Good idea. I'll get the plates," Gayle replied sounding as if she were in complete control of her emotions.

Once they were in the kitchen mother and daughter moved around the space without much conversation. This was in spite of the fact that what had happened screamed out for a discussion. At the very least it was something that should not be ignored.

"Do you think your dad would like another cup of coffee?" Gayle could hear and feel the trembling in her voice when she spoke.

"Mom," Victoria said with a sense of exasperation.

"You know that we can't' simply ignore what happened out there tonight," Victoria said as she pointed in the direction of the living room.

"Dad was always as sharp as ever. Under normal circumstances he would never make a mistake like that. To be honest mom I can't remember the last time dad failed to string his thoughts together. What we saw out there appeared to be a total melt down. You could see that dad had no recollection of Aunt Janice," Victoria said. She was slightly angry that her mother failed to acknowledge the obvious.

"Your father had a rough couple of days that's all," Gayle said in a dismissive manner.

"He's slowing down and that really bothers him. You know how men are when they get to a certain age. Only Heaven knows why but they all seem to fall apart at times. There's nothing to worry about Vicky. Your dad is fine," Gayle said. However, the nervous laugh which followed told Victoria that her mother was not as confident in her assessment as she attempted to project.

Victoria could tell that mom was making excuses for dad. She had trouble deciding if mom were covering for dad as a father or as the husband whom she swore to protect, love and respect.

"Hey what are you two doing in there? I'm beginning to feel abandoned," Wesley called out.

Victoria took note of the clear command that her dad had in his voice.

"Hold your cotton-picking horses," Gayle shot back. "We'll be there in just a minute."

Victoria would have given anything in the world to change what had happened. If she had not invited herself over with the offer of dinner or the mention of Aunt Janice, the events leading to dad's mishap would not have occurred. But on the other hand, Victoria knew that it made no sense beating herself up over something that was out of her control. Mom did say that dad was simply experiencing a couple of bad days.

That was not unusual.

But what if she were wrong and there was something more to what happened? Tonight was all about moving forward and getting dad all the help he may need. No small feat Victoria thought. Dad was as proud as he was stubborn.

Victoria spent the next few hours lying awake in bed thinking about her parents. She wanted to call and speak to her mother but was unsure what to say. Most of what she felt had already been covered. However, she understood that at some point the two of them would have to openly talk about the evening. Warts and all.

Monday morning.

After Victoria saw Jasmine board the school bus, she decided to have a cup of coffee before heading into the city. Operating on less than six hours of sleep was not her idea of fun. If nothing else the liquid refresher should help her remain alert throughout the first half of the day. By then Victoria was sure her second wind would have kicked in.

Hopefully there would be no surprises and the next eight hours would quietly fly by.

Instead of the smooth sailing, Victoria was informed that there would be a conference call with the Scottsdale, Arizona office this afternoon. The topic was Downing Sports. Victoria heard some talk about a departure from the advertising plan her team submitted weeks ago.

Victoria had dismissed the rumors…until now.

"Rick my team finished putting together several video proposals and sent it up the chain for review and approval. I expect to hear back from Tom Becker in the next day or so," Victoria said.

"I can appreciate that but the bottom line is that your people are the best at what they do and you can take full credit for that. Everyone knows that. It's not a matter of my or anyone else attempting to inflate your ego. That has nothing to do with it. To be open and honest I heard from Tom and he agrees that there needs to be some minor changes to the second and third videos, Rick said."

"Tom feels that the overall message from an advertising point needs to come across a bit stronger and cast a wider net if you will," Rick said.

Taking in the comments there was a tone of annoyance and disbelief in Victoria's voice when she responded.

"Tell you what Rick, let me get everyone together and we'll talk it over. I'm sure they'll view the news as the golden opportunity it appears to be," Victoria said through a level of controlled anger.

"That's fine. But we do need to put a bit of a rush on things," Rick said not wishing to add fuel to the fire that was noticeable in Victoria's response.

Five minutes later Victoria was back in her office sitting behind her desk taking in the conversation she just had. Once Victoria had time to cool off, she understood that this was not Rick's fault. He was simply the messenger. If it were anyone else Victoria would see it as the attempt to inflate an ego in the guise of having their own agenda pushed forward.

However, with Rick, Victoria knew that he was never one to play mind games. As long as she had known him deception was not something that he used to motivate any of his colleagues.

Victoria gathered everyone in the conference room and summarized the conversation she had with Rick. There were a smattering of groans and looks of anguish that Victoria chose to ignore. Victoria reminded everyone that while she believed they had done an excellent job, second opinions were a dime a dozen and should have been expected.

"Take it from me. Creative ideas no matter how well conceived never get an immediate rubber stamp of approval. I've been there and have come through unscathed and so will you," Victoria announced.

Victoria firmly believed in the conviction of her words and this was not some sugar-coated pep talk to the troops. Mission accomplished Victoria told herself once she got back to her office. She picked up the phone and began making the necessary calls to get their new plan of action underway.

With Wesley out of the house Gayle had the place all to herself. She began her daily cleaning routine starting in the kitchen then moving to the living room and finally Gayle made her way up to the second floor.

As usual Wesley left articles of his clothing on the bedroom and bathroom floors. This was a habit that she never convinced him to drop. Years of marriage or any amount of sweet talk notwithstanding.

With a dash of humor in mind Gayle hoped that perhaps one day Wesley may surprise her by doing exactly what she wanted when it came to picking up after himself. But for now, she had to lovingly deal with the man's shortcomings.

An hour after cleaning fatigue began to set in. Gayle had somewhat of a restless night even after consuming two cups of tea. Easy Sleep was the brand name of the beverage. Talk about a bait and switch Gayle thought to herself. The dream like music and the actor sleeping peacefully after consuming the tea was in sharp contrast to her reality.

Gayle went back downstairs to await her husband's arrival. She lowered her tired frame on to the couch with the television remote control in her left hand. One of her favorite soap operas were ten minutes from beginning. Gayle flipped through the channels finding there were an assortment of infomercials on just about each one. Gayle hated the prompted cheers of approval from the audience each time the host mentioned the wonders of product they were pitching. She imagined a sign going off just out of the cameras range when the producers wanted the audience to react. Gayle wondered how much each member of the audience was paid for their Hollywood style performance. Gayle swore that no matter how much the producers offered, she would never stoop to that level. Well, maybe if a trip to Paris were on the table, she would sing a different tune. The possibility brought a smile to Gayle's face.

According to the note Wesley left he went to the hardware store to pick up some supplies to repair the fence in the backyard. Gayle wondered what got into his head that caused him to tackle a job he had put off for the longest time.

The hardware store was only a ten-minute walk from the house and it was well past one two' clock. What could be keeping that man? Gayle was worried more now than she had ever been in the past.

Especially after what happened last night and the defense she put up when Victoria began asking questions about her father's mental state. By the time two-thirty rolled around Gayle couldn't wait any longer. She dialed Victoria's office number only to get her voice mail. She tried Victoria's cell number and on the second ring it was answered.

"Hey mom. What's up?" Victoria asked.

Gayle got right to the point of her call. In a hurried tone she informed Victoria that her father was missing.

The revelation was met with a cold silence for several seconds.

"I don't mean missing in the sense that someone has taken him. I mean he's been gone for most of the day and I haven't heard a word from him. I don't want to sound like a worrying old lady, but . . ." Gayle choked off the remainder of her sentence.

With everything that had gone on this morning this was the worst thing that could have happened Victoria thought. But she had to put that aside for the time being.

This situation was about family.

"Okay take it easy mom. When was the last time you spoke to dad?" Victoria asked attempting to remain as calm as she suggested her mother should be.

"Earlier he left a note saying that he was going to the hardware store to pick up a couple of things he needed to work in the backyard," Gayle responded in an unsteady tone.

"Did you call the hardware store and ask if he was there or try to call any of his friends?" Victoria asked.

In her state of panic Gayle hadn't thought about calling Wesley's best friend Russell.

Wesley was not very fond of those big hardware chains. He was more of a mom-and-pop kind of guy when it came to certain things.

He believed that those oversized outlets were corporate monsters. They took too much from working families who were trying to make the best of a bad situation. Wesley would not support them if his life depended on it. Wesley had been getting his supplies from Russell for the better part of twenty years and there was no indication that he would ever stop.

"No I didn't call the store, but that's a great place to start," Gayle said.

"That's okay mom you did the right thing by calling me. I just left the office and I'm on my way over. I should be there in about an hour and we'll both sit down and figure this whole thing out," Victoria said.

Victoria tried to remain calm and keep her emotions in check after hearing the panic in her mother's voice. Victoria heard stories about elderly people walking off and then turning up in the oddest places with no memory of what had happened. But was that dad? He had no history of that type of behavior. Victoria hoped to find her answer once she arrived at her parent's house.

As she crossed the bridge into Brooklyn Victoria was not sure what she was going to say to her mother. She understood that it was important to keep mom calm and focused. Victoria knew her mother as someone who had the ability to keep their emotions in check during a time of crisis. Yet in a situation like this you never know how a person is going to react and that included mom.

As Victoria maneuvered in and out of traffic, she prayed that dad was okay. In her mind Victoria saw her father at home safe and sound. Mom would be lecturing him about never leaving the house again without letting her know where he was going.

However.

"Vicky where are you?" her mother as asked in a hurried voice.

"Your father hasn't come home yet."

"I just crossed over into Brooklyn so I should be there in about a half an hour," Victoria responded while reminding herself to heed her own words about remaining calm.

"Just hurry," Gayle said without any concern if Victoria noticed the panic in her voice. This was not the time to play the brave little soldier and pretend that nothing had gone wrong. Although as a wife and mother she had to get herself together. That started by at least looking the part.

Gayle went upstairs and changed her clothes and removed the curlers from her hair and pulling and pinning it back. Victoria would be here in a little while and Gayle certainly did not want to look the part of a worried woman in distress.

Twenty-five minutes later.

"Mom," Victoria called out as she came through the front door.

"I'm upstairs. I'll be down in just a minute," Gayle called back.

Ten minutes later Gayle joined her daughter in the kitchen. Victoria had made herself a cup of tea and was seated at the small table adjacent to the stainless steel refrigerator.

"Now mom tell me everything that happened, starting with last night," Victoria began.

Gayle held nothing back just as Victoria requested. She even threw in the part where she threatened to send Wesley to the spare bedroom if he didn't control his snoring. Gayle promised herself that she would buy some of those strips to open the offender's nasal passage but each time it slipped her mind. Perhaps she should write it down and not leave it up to her memory.

Just as Victoria was about to say something in response to her mother's comments there was a familiar sound at the front door. It was a sound that both women had lived with for the better part of their lives. The whistled tune was unknown yet unmistakable.

Gayle literally jumped out of her chair and sprinted toward the front door with Victoria close behind. She had never seen her mother move so fast. However, these were extreme circumstances and a truck load of "firsts" were expected to occur, both positive and negative in the same breath.

When Wesley looked up after removing his shoes Gayle was standing inches from his chest. Without any words she pulled him into her arms as if he were a long lost relative that she had not seen in years.

"What is this all about?" Wesley innocently asked.

"Where have you been all day?" Gayle asked once she caught her breath.

Victoria remained silent watching the scene unfolding in front of her. She noticed the blank stare on her father's face as if he had no idea what his wife was referring too.

"I went to the hardware store to pick up a couple of things to finally repair that fence in the backyard," Wesley responded with a note of pride in his voice.

Victoria was the first one to notice, but she was not sure if she should say anything. If she gave a voice to the thoughts that were running around in her head it would challenge her father's explanation. But Victoria believed she had earned the right to question dad when something bothered her. Or had she?

Victoria wished she could plant her thoughts into her mother's head. Only mom could get away with questioning dad unscathed.

Victoria studied her mother in the hope that she would say something. At least demand a legitimate explanation from dad for his absence. However, it appeared that mom was so glad to have him safe and back home she made no mention of the fact that his hands were almost empty. Dad had a clear plastic shopping bag in his hand but it contained a single item—a hammer.

The issue that Victoria struggled with was asking her dad to produce the "couple of things" that he picked up. But even if he produced an arm full of purchases it would not explain the length of his absence that mom described.

Victoria could not hold back any longer.

"But dad," Victoria began. "Where are all of the things that you bought?"

In a physical response to the question Wesley's forehead creased. His mind worked as if searching for the answer to a complicated equation.

As he thought about the question Wesley's mind struggled in search of an answer that would satisfy both women. More importantly, an answer that he could accept for himself.

"Umm . . ." was all he could manage.

"That's all right," Gayle began. "As long as you're home. Thank God for that."

Gayle took her husband's arm and led him toward the kitchen choosing to ignore Victoria's question. However, she could not dismiss the fact that Wesley had no answer to Victoria's question. Gayle decided that she would seek a response when the time was right and not before.

It was a bright Saturday morning and for the past three days the only thing Jasmine could think about was what her grandparents bought for her birthday.

"Mom, do you know what grandma and grandpa got for my birthday?"

"They would only say that it was something special," Victoria responded flatly.

Jasmine looked up from her plate of food wondering if her mom was holding something back.

"Maybe it's that electronic game I wanted," Jasmine guessed.

"Maybe," Victoria answered.

"We'll have to wait and see. But first you have to finish your breakfast and start working on that book report that's due."

Jasmine could not hide the look of disappointment that appeared on her face. School work was the last thing she wanted to think about—especially on a day like today.

"But mom," Jasmine began in protest.

"We also have to stop by the library," Victoria added—a fact that only compounded Jasmine's misery.

The morning had rolled past before Victoria realized the time. It was almost one o'clock and her parents wanted Victoria to bring Jasmine over around three o'clock. Victoria had no idea what they would do to kill the next few hours. However, when shopping was not on the table there was always the next best thing.

"How about a trip to the hairdresser?" Victoria asked.

"Really?" Jasmine asked in a tone as if to question the sincerity of her mother's offer.

"Why not," Victoria responded with conviction.

"Your hair could use a little trimming," Victoria added.

Jasmine stopped manipulating the electronic game she had been playing and ran her fingers through her hair as if that would confirm her mother's words.

"Can we go to Gloria's?" Jasmine asked.

"Let me give her a call. I know we don't have an appointment but since it's your birthday she might make an exception," Victoria said.

With thirty minutes to spare Victoria and Jasmine had their new looks completed and were on the way to celebrate a birthday for one deserving young lady.

Just as they were pulling into the driveway Jasmine put her game away. There was a smile on her face that could brighten any day of the week. Jasmine looked so happy right now and Victoria wished that she could bottle the moment and save it forever.

"How do I look mom?" Jasmine asked.

"Did my hair get messed up?'

"Don't worry honey you look great," Victoria responded.

"Are you sure?" Jasmine pressed.

"The belle of the ball," Victoria replied with a smile of her own.

As mother and daughter walked up the driveway drawing closer to the house, they noticed several helium balloons tied to the lamp post on either side of the front door. The balloons bore the message *'Happy Birthday Jasmine.'*

Just as Victoria was about to insert her key into the lock her mother opened the door.

"Happy birthday," Gayle shouted as she bent down and scooped Jasmine up and into her arms. Victoria knew that her mother suffered with arthritis but at the moment you would never know it.

"Hi grandma," Jasmine said as she held on tight.

"Come on in and let's get this party started," Gayle cheerfully ordered.

"I'm all for that," Victoria added. "Where's dad?" she asked as she passed through the front door.

"The last time I saw him he was upstairs getting dressed. He said something about looking sharp for a special occasion," Gayle offered.

"Leave it to dad to always be the ham in the act," Victoria jokingly said.

As they walked into the living room Victoria was surprised to see more balloons and decorations. Jasmine's face told the story of her being very impressed. There were balloons with the faces of her favorite cartoon characters on them. To her left Jasmine noticed a mountain of presents.

"Are all of those for me?" Jasmine asked in a voice that said she could not believe what her eyes were seeing.

"We'll have to take back whatever you can't open," Wesley said as he entered the living room.

"Happy birthday," he said. Wesley's voice boomed and seemed to fill every corner of the space. At the sight of her grandfather Jasmine ran across the room and jumped into Wesley's open arms. He spun Jasmine around three full times before putting her back down.

"Can I start opening the presents now Grandma?" Jasmine asked with the unrestrained eagerness of a child.

"Wouldn't you like to open your cards first?" Gayle asked.

"No way," Jasmine responded as she eagerly rubbed the palms of her hands together.

"You know how she is when it comes to opening presents. There's no stopping her," Victoria said as a matter of fact.

"You might as well go for it," Wesley threw in for good measure.

"Cards are just cards, but presents are presents," he added with emphasis.

"You can open and read your cards while we're having dessert."

Victoria didn't agree with her dad's suggestion but decided to let it pass. There was no real harm in opening presents before you read the card of the gift giver, but it was a matter of protocol. Lighten up Victoria silently chastised herself. Everyone else was having a good time and here you are stuck on protocol. Shame on you Victoria thought to herself.

The adults in the room watched as Jasmine tore through the wrapping paper exposing gift after gift. Her expression of joy and delight rose as she opened each one.

Jasmine was down to the last three gifts. Victoria wondered what Jasmine's reaction would be if the gift she wanted most was not there. The situation almost resembled one of those game shows that her mom watched. The contestant was asked to choose between one of three curtains. One would be empty, the next would contain what can be best described as a booby prize and the last would contain the grand prize.

Victoria hoped her parents were able to find the gift that Jasmine wanted. Victoria watched as Jasmine opened the first box.

Not that one.

They all watched as Jasmine picked up and vigorously shook the second gift.

"Take it easy there gunslinger," Wesley humorously cautioned. "You don't want to break whatever is inside, do you?"

Jasmine let loose a high-pitched laugh in response.

The next gift Jasmine revealed were a pair of sneakers. Pink and white. They were the latest fashion that all of the girls in Jasmine's peer group were wearing.

As Jasmine picked up the last present Victoria discretely crossed her fingers. She wondered what was going through her daughter's mind as she tore the wrapping paper from the box.

It was then that Jasmine squealed with delight. She had gotten the gift of all gifts. In her excitement Jasmine danced around in circles before speaking.

"Cool," was the first that spilled out.

"Thank you grandma and grandpa. This is the best. The best," she said once again, clearly unable to control her emotions. The gift was an electronic game that just hit the market called 'Just for the Girls.' The game was a sports-based theme, where girls competed against girls from across the country. The leader would choose the sport and her team.

"Mom look what grandma and grandpa got for me."

Jasmine leapt into her grandparent's open arms. As the trio embraced a look of joy and satisfaction raced across Victoria's face. Thank goodness her parents came through. On the sly Victoria flashed the thumbs up sign in their direction.

"All right. Who's in the mood for cake and ice cream?" Gayle announced.

"I am," Jasmine and her grandfather said together.

"Vicky want to give me a hand in the kitchen?" Gayle asked.

"Of course. All right you two don't go anywhere, we'll be right back," Victoria said.

While Victoria and Gayle were in the kitchen setting up dessert Jasmine began to open her birthday cards. There was one from Aunt Rose and Uncle Gregory who lived in Florida. The card contained two crisp twenty-dollar bills.

"I'm rich," Jasmine shouted as she waved the two bills in the air.

The next envelope that Jasmine picked up had drawings on the front and back with the name Christine written on it. Jasmine turned the card over several times. She was not sure what to do next and looked to her grandfather for his guidance in response to the puzzled look on her face.

"It's all right sweetheart," Wesley said as he took in Jasmine's hesitation.

"It's from me," he said with the pride of a first-time grandparent.

"But grandpa . . ." Jasmine said with a clear tone of doubt in her voice. Although he had given her permission to open the envelope, Jasmine was not sure if she really should proceed. The envelope did not have her name on it, but she did as she was told. When Jasmine opened and read the card her confusion elevated. Who in the world was Christine she wondered?

Wesley had a look of joy on his face as he watched his granddaughter hold the card loosely in her hand.

"What's going on out there?" Gayle called out from the kitchen. "It's awfully quiet."

"It's okay," Wesley responded. "Jasmine just opened the card that I gave her."

Jasmine knew there was something wrong. Why would grandpa give her a birthday card with the name Christine on it? In her mind Jasmine turned the question over and over. She failed to come up with a reason that she could understand. Perhaps grandpa was playing a joke on her. But that didn't make any sense Jasmine reasoned. Maybe she should just ask him. That's what mom always said you should do when something bothered you. It was the best way to get the answer you were looking for and then there would be no mistakes.

But this was her grandpa.

However just before Jasmine made up her mind, Gayle and Victoria entered the room with dessert. Victoria brought in Jasmine's favorite. A double frosted chocolate cake adorned with multi-colored long-stemmed candles.

"Get the lights," Gayle called out.

After the lights were turned off the living room was bathed in a yellowish flickering glow. The sparkle from the flame added a whimsical effect to the room. After leading everyone in two rounds of the happy birthday song it was time for Jasmine to make her wish. Jasmine thought for a moment before blowing out all of the candles on the cake. However, everyone got a good laugh when the candles unexpectedly reignited brighter than before.

"You gotta try harder next time," Wesley offered in an encouraging tone.

Once again Jasmine inhaled and exhaled. But seconds later the same thing happened.

"Hey no fair mom," Jasmine shouted. "Those are trick candles."

"All right. This time we'll all make a wish and blow them out Victoria responded in Jasmine's direction.

For the next two hours the family played board games and in honor of the day Jasmine won her fair share. They sang songs and were entertained by a few of Wesley's magic tricks that were always a big hit with Jasmine.

After a while it was obvious that Jasmine had run out of steam. Victoria escorted Jasmine upstairs to the bedroom where she had grown up. Victoria noticed that mom and dad had not made many changes over the years. Victoria's dresser was still there as were most of her dolls and stuffed animals. Victoria thought mom would have turned the room into a getaway space. Maybe a place where she could shut out the world and focus on her creative side. Sewing and craft making were a specialty of hers. Victoria recalled how mom used to make things for everyone in the family. Especially at Christmas time. As far as Victoria could remember there was not a family member who didn't have something that was handmade by mom. Whether it was an embroidered scarf, a handkerchief or a quilt, her skills were always well received and appreciated. Victoria understood that the apple had indeed fallen far from the tree with respect to crafting. She could barely get a line of thread through the eye of a needle. Victoria realized that without the services of her tailor she'd be lost.

Just as Victoria was about to leave Jasmine's voice pierced the silence. Jasmine spoke in a soft tone as if she were about to reveal the secrets of life itself.

"You want to know something strange mom?" Jasmine began with the back of her right hand touching the opposite corner of her lip. "Grandpa made a big mistake before."

A puzzled look appeared on Victoria's face.

"What do you mean honey?" Victoria asked hoping it was nothing serious. What children took as being alarming in their limited world usually amounted to nothing at all in the grand scheme of things. Jasmine was no exception in that regard.

"Grandpa put a different name on my birthday card. He wrote the name Christine," Jasmine said still confused by the obvious mistake.

Victoria was not sure how to respond to her daughter's revelation. In a word she was dumbfounded. If she were not worried about dad when he took his "trip," she definitely had a reason to worry about him now. This was nothing like forgetting where you left your keys or the right day of the week. Forgetting the name of your only grandchild was a serious issue.

"Are you sure?" Victoria asked with some measure of doubt riding on her words.

"Grandpa could never forget your name," Victoria added.

Jasmine waited patiently for her mother to say something else.

"Where's the card now?" Victoria asked.

"I left it on the table with the rest the cards. Look at it and you'll see," Jasmine said in defense of what she knew to be true.

"Okay. I'll check it out later. But now it's time for you to get some sleep. We have a long ride back home." Victoria said as she turned to leave the bedroom once again.

While going down stairs Victoria thought about Jasmine's words. Although dad was not the rock of the family that mom was, if there were something seriously wrong with dad would she be up to keeping that crown? The possibility that she could not bothered Victoria more than she cared to recognize.

When Victoria entered the living room dad was sitting in front of the television while the news played. Victoria paused momentarily and listened to his heavy breathing. There was a magazine in his hands and he was flipping through page after page without paying much attention to any particular article.

"Is she asleep?" Wesley asked without turning to look in Victoria's direction.

"Not yet, but she's on her way," Victoria responded.

"Hmmm," Wesley offered as his only means of acknowledgement.

"Where's mom?" Victoria asked.

Wesley pointed over his left shoulder.

As Victoria entered the kitchen her mother was loading the dishwasher. Victoria watched as she rinsed each plate before placing it inside the machine. The exercise seemed redundant but Victoria chose not to judge.

"Mom, I have to talk to you about something." Victoria's voice was choppy at best.

"What is it honey?" Gayle asked.

"It's about dad."

"Yes," Gayle said in response.

"Jasmine said that dad wrote someone else's name on her birthday card."

Gayle didn't immediately respond. Her face was emotionless when she finally looked in her daughter's direction.

"What do you mean he wrote the wrong name in the card? There has to be some kind of mistake. Is Jasmine sure about that? It's not possible that her grandfather would make that kind of error. No way," Gayle said.

Victoria did not want to get into an argument with her mother. Especially on a day like today.

"Jasmine said that she left the card on the table with her gifts," Victoria offered in a tone that said her mother should look at the evidence and see for herself.

"Did you say anything to your father or look at the card for yourself?" Gayle asked.

Victoria did not have much of a choice when she responded negatively to both questions.

"Well don't. I'll talk to him about it later. Right now is not the time to bring something like that up. He's happy and I don't want to spoil the mood," Gayle said in somewhat of a commanding tone.

Victoria could not help the feeling of being annoyed at her mother's stance on something so important.

"Mom, I think this is something we have to discuss. What if dad starts to forget other things? Important things. Not remembering his grandchild's name could be the tip of the iceberg so to speak," Victoria pressed.

Gayle listened intently to her daughter but remained silent. The allegation that there might be something mentally wrong with her father was nothing short of a slap in the face.

Victoria hated to ask and the words were almost choked back down her throat. But the question had to be posed.

"Mom when was the last time dad had a complete physical examination?" Victoria asked.

"What do you mean by that?" Gayle asked. She was standing just inches from Victoria with a dish cloth in her hands that she unfolded and refolded again. It was a clear sign of her nervousness and not being aware of her actions.

"I don't mean to sound disrespectful mom but I think you know what I mean," Victoria responded. "After what happened the other day, we need to be concerned. Right?"

"I think you should let me handle this in my own way and in my own time," Gayle responded. Her voice displayed a wave of anger that Victoria had not witnessed in years. As far as she knew mom was always the level headed one while dad had a tendency to fly off the handle every now and then.

But mom . . . never.

"Maybe you're right. But the sooner you talk to dad about it the better," Victoria offered attempting to stem a potential argument. Yet she wondered if there were other instances of dad's forgetfulness that mom knew about but chose to keep secret. Suppose he went for a drive and got into an accident or left something on the stove and caused a fire. His absentmindedness could bring unintentional harm to mom as well as to himself. Victoria believed that she would have a hard time in forgiving herself for not addressing the problem much earlier in spite of her mother's feelings.

Victoria also wondered how much blame she should place on her mother. Victoria also had to consider the ramifications if dad experienced one of his episodes while he was out with Jasmine.

"But mom," Victoria began before being cut off.

"I said that I'll take care of it and I will," Gayle snapped at Victoria.

"I don't want to hear another word about it," Gayle added. There was a mask of anger on her face. The emotional outburst was as unfamiliar to her as it was to Victoria and neither one knew how it would end. It was as if the two women were facing a political standoff with neither one willing to give into the other's convictions. Each believed that they knew what was best for the man they loved. Victoria felt this was not the time or the place to play the role of the dutiful daughter and acquiesce to her mother's feelings. Especially one that would impact the entire family.

Jasmine was a child and she would not understand what was happening to her grandfather. Whether Victoria liked it or not Jasmine was involved just as much as everyone else in the family.

During the ride home Jasmine didn't have much to say. Thankfully she was focused on the gifts from her grandparents. Victoria took her preoccupation as a present of her own. She was not up to answering questions at the moment.

Victoria's thoughts switched gears and she focused on the fact that she had to go out of town on business next week. Jasmine had the week off from school and Victoria was worried about her staying with mom and dad. With mom appearing to be wearing a set of blinders when it came to dad there was a reason to be concerned. Victoria needed someone to talk too—not a family member and certainly not a "professional," but simply a friend. It had to be someone she respected and valued their opinion. Victoria decided she would take care of that on Monday morning.

Gayle sat at the vanity table in their bedroom absently brushing her hair. This was a nightly ritual ever since she graduated from high school. Gayle's back was to Wesley who was propped up in bed with the television remote control in hand. He went through station after station in search of something that would hold his interest. Gayle hated watching television with Wesley because he rarely watched any one program to its entirety—except sports. However, when asked, Wesley could recite chapter and verse of the program he started out watching. Gayle thought about hiding the remote but decided that would be cruel.

"Our grandchild is growing up to be quite a lady," Wesley blurted out.

"Pretty soon she'll be dating and driving," he added.

"Hmmm," Gayle offered in response.

She had just finished brushing her hair and completed the exercise by pulling it back and tying a ribbon to the extended pony tail. The streaks of gray hair against the natural dark color gave Gayle a distinguished and striking appearance. Although she had grayed prematurely in life that did nothing to detract from her beauty.

"Now that's not much of an answer," Wesley said with a sense of disappointment in his voice.

"I'm sorry," Gayle said. "I was thinking about Vicky. You're right Jasmine is growing up fast. But that part about her driving and dating is something I'm sure your daughter is not looking forward to facing. Kids like Jasmine seem to be growing up too fast anyway," Gayle said sadly.

Although Wesley was silent, he was no longer focused on the remote control or the television set.

Gayle continued her thought.

"With all of the technology being thrown at them young people have no time to enjoy being kids," Gayle offered once again. Her sense of sorrow for Jasmine's generation was clear.

"You have to remember that life is nothing like it was when we were Jasmine's age. This generation seems to live life on cruise control," Wesley offered.

Gayle joined Wesley in bed and slipped beneath the covers.

"Do you think Vicky is happy with her life right now?" Gayle asked while looking into Wesley's eyes.

"What do you mean by that?" Wesley asked.

"You know what I mean," Gayle responded.

"She's a successful career woman raising a child on her own. Everyone knows that the two lifestyles rarely go on merrily hand in hand. Think oil and vinegar," Gayle said with a tone of doom and gloom in her voice.

When Wesley did not respond, Gayle continued as if giving a legal summation in court.

"What I'm saying is that the two opposing lifestyles can take a toll on anyone. Even if they try to hide it from the outside world or those closest to the individual. Stress like that can make a person see things that are not necessarily there and jump to the wrong conclusions. I've seen it happen and so have you. This is something that I want our daughter to avoid at all costs. Don't you agree?" Gayle offered.

Unknown to Wesley, Gayle was taking a shot at Victoria's comments regarding his mental health.

Wesley took a moment to consider his wife's concerns. Gayle was not the type of person to speak without having all of the facts to back up her beliefs. In this case, it was as if she had some inside information concerning Victoria that he was not privy too.

Wesley understood that mothers and daughters had heart to heart talks all of the time, with subjects ranging from A to Z. Yet he never got the feeling that Vicky was unhappy with her life or the choices she made since becoming a widow and a single parent. Wesley couldn't help but wonder where Gayle was going with her as of now, unfounded concerns.

Wesley got the sense that Gayle was leading him down a path he did not necessarily want to travel. The fact that Vicky chose not to date much after Raymond's passing never bothered him to the point where he became worried about her future or her emotional state. He reasoned that Vicky needed some personal space as a woman and more importantly as a mother. Their daughter was strong enough to handle any and all issues when it came to matters of the heart and career. That being said, Wesley realized there were times when he was on the outside looking in, but it was never a matter of disrespect by either his wife or daughter.

"I think Vicky's enjoying her life and managing it the best way she can. She's got a beautiful child to teach and take care of and two of the best parents under the sun. What else can any daughter want?" Wesley said in an attempt to lighten the mood.

"You may be right but don't you think it's time Vicky started dating again?" Gayle asked in a manner meant to solicit Wesley's agreement.

Wesley moved in closer and lovingly held Gayle's hand before he continued to give his opinion where Vicky's personal life was concerned.

"Vicky will be able to lean on us if and when the time came. But we are not going to be around forever and like you said Jasmine is growing like a weed. The little girl that we used to hold in our arms is becoming an individual right before our eyes. Understand that we've done our best at teaching Victoria how life works, while letting her succeed or fail at her own pace. That's as important as anything we may have taught her," Wesley said.

During their years of marriage Wesley knew when to keep his mouth shut and not get into a debate with his wife. But this was not one of those times. Wesley was free to offer his opinion and set his wife's mind at ease when it came to the welfare of their daughter.

He must have succeeded because without another word Gayle gave him kiss on the lips and turned over to her side of the bed, which in effect said the discussion was over.

Victoria entered Sharon's office with a look on her face that said she was ready to bear her soul. Her legs felt as if they were encased in cement as she moved.

Sharon always had an open ear whenever Victoria needed one and hopefully this was one of those times.

Victoria began by talking about the trip she and her team were about to take this week. Over the years Sharon had done her fair share of flying across the country for business and for the most part she was not a fan of the idea.

After several minutes of round about chatter Sharon tactfully requested that Victoria to get to the point of her visit.

"All right Victoria out with it. We've known each other long enough for me to see when something is bothering you. The conversation about work was just fluff. I know you didn't come in here this early in the morning to discuss your business schedule," Sharon firmly said.

Before beginning to speak Victoria exhaled loudly expressing the sense of frustration brewing inside.

"Don't you ever get tired of being right?" Victoria asked with a smile on her face.

"If you throw in the word always, then the answer is no," Sharon responded in appreciation of Victoria's flattering remark.

"It's my dad," Victoria said. There was a slight yet noticeable hesitation before she continued.

"Lately he's been forgetting the simplest things. For instance, about a week ago he left the house for hours. My mother was worried sick. When he finally showed up, he basically had no idea where he had gone. He said something about going to the hardware store to pick up a couple of things but when . . ."

Victoria had stopped in the middle of her revelation not sure if she should continue due to a feeling of embarrassment on her part and that of her father.

However, Sharon helped with that.

"Go on," Sharon urged.

"When I asked him where the items he bought were, he had no answer," Victoria offered.

Sharon said nothing in response. She adjusted her body in the chair as if waiting for the second shoe to drop.

Victoria continued with her story.

"It was Jasmine's birthday, and dad signed someone else's name on the card. I told my mother about it and she became unusually defensive. I've never seen her react that way about anything," Victoria said. Her words had a tone of hurt and anger at the same time.

Sharon could see that opening up about these events were difficult for Victoria. She knew from meeting Victoria's parents years ago; they were a close-knit family and it was hard for her to believe Victoria's mother would react that way.

Sharon was silent for a moment. She had a secret of her own when it came to an aging parent. Sharon thought about the trauma her family went through when her mother began showing signs of mental depreciation. The affliction ultimately led to her mother being hospitalized. Over the years it was Sharon's cross to bear and she chose to remain silent. But as the years went by, she was able to open up about her past when the time was right.

"This is something that I haven't thought about or spoke about in a very long time. So much to the point where I try to forget that it ever happened. I know exactly what you're going through. I'm sure you've heard those words more times than you care to remember. But I mean it. Several years ago, my mother had problems of her own that affected the entire family."

Finally, a kindred spirit Victoria excitedly thought.

"I'm sorry to hear that. I had no idea that you were dealing with your own family situation," Victoria said with a genuine sense of sorrow.

"Thanks. But that was long time ago. Yet at the same time it is something that I will never forget," Sharon said.

"While I suffered on a personal level, I managed to pull myself up from the doldrums and get my act together," Sharon offered with a sense of achievement.

Sharon was not bragging about getting her life back on track. She was speaking to a friend hoping that her words offered some encouragement that Victoria was more than capable of doing the very same thing.

"I'm going to be straight forward with you Victoria. You need to iron out things with your mother. The last thing either one of you want is a broken relationship," Sharon said indicating that her words should not be taken lightly.

Sharon took a moment to study Victoria's face and to let her words sink in before she continued.

"Things can be said between family members in the heat of the moment that can do irreparable harm. The saying about time healing all wounds can only carry you so far. I think your mother will come to realize that your dad is changing and may need professional help. She also has to come to grips with the fact that her lifelong partner may be slipping. As painful as it may be, your dad's fading memory will include past events and people that have surrounded him for most of his life. You guys are going to have to act as coach and mentor at the same time."

Sharon spoke with a sense of wisdom and experience in the same voice. Victoria found herself totally absorbed in her words. Victoria felt as if she were a child and Sharon played the role of a mother providing crucial life advice to someone that had not lived a life of their own.

"That may not be as easy as you make it sound," Victoria responded as if caught in the grip of a lost cause.

"Fair enough. You make good point" Sharon said.

"Try waking up one day and finding out that a loved one can't remember who you are. Nothing in life can prepare you for something like that," Victoria lamented.

With interlocked fingers Sharon stretched her arms across the desk in Victoria's direction.

"Listen, emotional turmoil can be one of the most devastating experiences to try and get over. The important thing is to not try and cure yourself by yourself. For whatever it's worth you did the right thing when you made the decision to walk through my door," Sharon said.

"Oh, it's like that huh? Presto-changeo, one-two-three and all will be right with the world once again," Victoria offered with a tone of skepticism.

Sharon looked at Victoria hoping she had gotten through to her. But if she failed Sharon had already decided that she would not give up or take a single step backward.

"Just remember what I said about reaching out for help. Keep that in mind and you'll have the battle won in no time at all," Sharon said.

The advice brought a smile of resolution that Victoria thought was not possible. Victoria realized that she had come to the right place at the right time. Hearing, but more importantly listening to another voice made all the difference in the world.

"Victoria, you have to keep in mind that everyone needs a little help every now and then and you're no exception to that rule. Remember, you have to surround yourself with people you believe can help. Strength in numbers Victoria. Always believe in the power of strength in numbers," Sharon pressed.

"Now, about that scarf you're wearing. It's fabulous. Where did you get it?" Sharon asked.

That night Victoria thought long and hard about Sharon's advice. Especially the part about patching things up with mom. On the way home she wanted to stop and call her but she kept pushing it aside for no good reason. However, that would change in the morning.

Jasmine had fallen asleep hours ago. Clothed in a world of innocent dreams conjured by a child's mind she was at peace. Now as the moments slipped away it was Victoria's turn to dream.

Victoria got to work until well after nine o'clock. Although she had gotten a decent night's sleep another couple of hours would have been a blessing from above.

Victoria entered her office and flicked on the light switch. She could still smell the faint trace of disinfectant used to clean lingering in the air. Once she was comfortably seated Victoria took a deep breath and focused her attention toward the telephone on her desk. She reached out for the device but then drew her hand back as if the phone were a snake that was about to strike.

"Oh, c'mon don't be such a chicken-shit," Victoria chastised herself. Now was as good a time as any to get the verbal ball rolling with mom. She punched in her parent's phone number on the keypad without any further hesitation.

Victoria started out by apologizing and confessing that her emotions had gotten the better of her the other day. Gayle also expressed a healthy measure of regret for her inability to react in a more civil manner.

Mother and daughter laughed, cried a little and laughed again.

Victoria was happy that mom came to the realization that dad needed help. At times dad would fight tooth and nails when it came to seeing a doctor. Unless he couldn't stand or eat dad would never admit there was a problem. Mom told stories where she had to almost drag dad to the doctor. As for him keeping an appointment that was a story for another day.

For the next two days Victoria focused on office matters. She had always used her career as a shield against the problems surrounding a personal life. She often joked about the fact that she really had no personal life to speak of outside of her family. Perhaps using her career in that manner was the reward that helped her succeed. In any event that was the way Victoria lived her life and she could not envision much of a change. On the other hand, Victoria had suffered through long sleepless nights wondering if she would ever fall in love again. It was not a matter of finding "Mr. Right," it was something entirely different. When Victoria stopped to think about her situation and as those around her that have moved on, she wondered if she could harness the same inner strength. Sharon was the face of that type of individual. Knowing what she knew about Sharon, Victoria realized that she could take a lesson or two as far as her career and as a daughter.

Victoria hated having these philosophical conversations with herself, but sometimes it couldn't be avoided.

Victoria arrived at her parent's house just before six o'clock. As she entered Victoria took note that things were unusually quiet. Mom and dad had to know she was coming over around this time. She wondered why neither one of them or Jasmine for that matter failed to greet her at the front door. Maybe they were out in the backyard relaxing. It was a beautiful day and at least another three hours of sunshine were promised by the metrological forecasters.

Victoria made her way through the living room and into the kitchen. In many homes the kitchen was the place where family and friends gathered. In many cultures it was believed to be the heart of the home. Besides being a place where meals were prepared it was the place where conversations began and opinions were expressed. The kitchen was also a place where tragedy and happiness at times clashed—and true to form the scene that met Victoria's eyes caused her to momentarily lose her breath. Her mother was seated at the counter crying. Although her hands covered a good portion of her face Victoria could see the stream of tears cascading down her cheeks.

Victoria froze in her tracks. She couldn't move her legs any further forward if she tried.

Victoria noticed that her mother's bible lay next to her. It was worn and ragged from time and use but she religiously carried it back and forth to church every Sunday. Gayle staunchly refused everyone's offer of a new one. Victoria remembered that growing up her mother would read a passage or two each night before putting her to bed. Back then Victoria had trouble understanding most of the words or their meaning. She recalled the look of annoyance and frustration on her mother's face when after every passage she would ask a new question.

When Victoria regained her motor function she cautiously approached.

"Mom?"

Her voice was filled with concern and a touch of fear. However, there was no answer or a sign of acknowledgement to her daughter's presence.

"Mom what's the matter?" Victoria asked as she gently placed her right hand on her mother's shoulder.

Without a word being said Gayle quickly rose from her seat and wrapped her arms around Victoria to the point where she almost lost her balance. It seemed as if time itself had stopped and started again before Gayle released her grip.

Again, Victoria asked her mother what was bothering her. But it was obvious that her emotional outburst had something to do with dad and from the look of things the news was not good.

Finally Gayle spoke.

"Dear God in Heaven I think I've lost him," Gayle said in sorrow.

Victoria guided her mother back to her seat and eased her down.

"What are you talking about mom?" Victoria asked.

"It's your father," Gayle managed in spite of the fact that she had not fully regained her composure. She wiped the tears from her eyes with the crumpled tissue that she held in her hand.

"What about dad, what's the matter mom?" Victoria asked this time with an increased sense of urgency in her voice.

"I don't understand what happened but for a moment your father had no idea who I was and he couldn't even remember his own granddaughter."

Gayle held the bible close to her chest in the hope of receiving some measure of solace and guidance.

"Slow down mom and tell me exactly what happened," Victoria said.

Gayle did not respond and her face was slightly contorted. It was as if her brain were processing a difficult mathematical equation instead of the simple request posed by her daughter.

Victoria pulled over a stool from the other side of the marble topped island and placed it directly in front of her mother. Victoria sat down and placed the palms of her hands on each one of her mother's shoulders.

"Take your time mom and try to remember everything." Victoria requested in an encouraging manner.

Gayle looked into her daughter's eyes and as difficult as it was, she began to unveil the source of her pain and anguish.

"The doctor said that your father is suffering from onset of Alzheimer's." Gayle heard the words coming from within yet the sound of her voice seemed as foreign as they were distant. It was as if someone else were speaking about a person unknown to her. This had nothing to do with her husband. Gayle refused to accept the reality of the situation in spite of the emotional turmoil that coursed through her body.

Victoria watched closely as her mother's sense of despair and grief changed to one of anger and contempt. Perhaps she was angry at life, maybe it was the doctor that diagnosed dad, or perhaps her anger was reserved for God Himself for letting something like this happen to her husband.

Victoria always thought of her mother as the driving force behind her parent's marriage. But now with dad's condition Victoria was left to question how this might affect their relationship. Beside the fact that dad would need mom's support now more than ever, Victoria wondered if mom were up to the task of taking on the role of wife and live-in care provider.

Victoria hadn't thought about it before but she took a moment to question her relationship with her father. As far back as her teenage years Victoria would seek out dad's advice related to things that were important to her. Boys were high on that list.

"Did you suggest that dad have a second opinion?" Victoria asked.

"Of course. The doctors went through a battery of tests and your father completed some but struggled with others. Especially the parts where his long-term memory were being challenged." There was such a sorrowful sound in Gayle's voice but she continued just the same.

"The doctor prescribed a number of medications that your father has to take on a daily basis and our only hope is to manage the situation as best as we can. The doctor said the family has to be as supportive as ever under the circumstances. He said your father would struggle putting his thoughts together at times, yet he would be lucid and engaging in others."

Gayle knew that no matter how much she tried to put on a brave face, she had to admit the man she'd spent the better part of her life with would slowly begin to change.

Victoria was so wrapped up in the moment that she forgot to ask her mother where dad was right now. Seconds later she posed the question.

"He's upstairs sleeping," Gayle responded. The tone in her voice indicated that she was glad that Wesley was not around. Gayle realized that knowing what she knew it would have been difficult to face him.

"Mom is there anything I can do to help?" Victoria asked noting the tremor in her voice.

"Besides praying and asking the good Lord to guide us through this awful trial, I can't think of anything more," Gayle responded.

Victoria reflected back on the fact that her mother always kept the bible close. Even when she was preparing for bed it was never out of reach. The bible was always opened to the 23rd Psalm and Victoria could not help but wonder if it gave mom a sense peace and comfort through the night.

If it hadn't in the past Victoria reasoned that after everything that happened today, mom would need every crutch available to her. The spiritual as well as the physical.

Victoria's thoughts turned to Jasmine and how she would process the news about her grandfather. Victoria wondered how she was going to tell Jasmine that her grandpa was ill and over time may become worse. How was she going to tell a child that the man she thought of as "Mr. Everything" may not be made of steel after all? When it boiled down to it Victoria had a hard time handling the hard cold reality of the situation herself. Would she be able to deal with the fact that dad may not recognize his family? That he may struggle to remember the simplest things in life. He may begin to have trouble recognizing faces in pictures and events that had occurred in the past. Victoria feared that from now on everything about the family would be different and not necessarily for the better. It was sad but Victoria had to deal with the fact that contrary to her mother's belief, God forgive her, prayer was not an answer to all of the ills the world had to offer.

"Mom, I have some personal time I can take off from work if you need me," Victoria offered.

"I don't think it's going to come to that," Gayle responded as she took a hold of her daughter's hands.

"Let's cross one bridge at a time okay," Gayle said attempting to sound as upbeat as possible.

"You have a life of your own to manage and you certainly can't spend that time looking after us. There's so much out there for you to deal with that doesn't include your parents. Remember, I've been taking care of your father and doing a pretty good job of it so I think I can manage this little set back," Gayle said in a boastful tone.

Victoria did not respond but she was glad to hear the positive change in her mother's voice and attitude when it came to dad. But she wondered what her mother meant about things being out there for her.

It was true that mom had taken care of dad for years on end but there was a time to be strong and exercise one's inner strength. But as Sharon had flatly expressed, there were times when even the strongest minded person needed a helping hand. There had to be an understanding that anyone couldn't fix everything no matter how hard they tried. While Victoria understood and appreciated her mother's stance, she hoped her offer of help was not dismissed without being considered.

"I'm going upstairs to check on Jasmine, but I'll be back in a moment and we can finish talking," Victoria said.

As quietly as possible Victoria opened the bedroom door and found that Jasmine was still asleep. Victoria took a moment to take in Jasmine's face. Innocence and admiration were the two words that came to mind.

Victoria watched as her child's eyes bounced from side to side beneath her eyelids. She wondered what stories of excitement and adventure swirled within Jasmine's mind as she dreamed. Victoria saw what appeared to be a smile form on Jasmine's face. There was no doubt she was having the time of her life…

…even if it were only in a dream.

Victoria had been told by some professionals and those in the know that dreams were often slices of reality containing past deeds and events yet to come. In her mind just how true that line of thinking was had yet to be confirmed. Victoria checked her watch and made the decision to let Jasmine sleep. There was no harm in letting her spend the night with her grandparents. The decision would give Victoria the opportunity to sort out her feelings about mom and dad. Victoria felt as if she were caught in a vacuum or worse, swimming against a raging tide without any form of rescue. But she also understood that this was no time to feel sorry for herself. Victoria realized that inner pity would be counter-productive and she would not be able to function at home or at work.

Over the years Victoria had expended much of her energy overcoming obstacles that were placed in front of her. To fall apart emotionally now would be disastrous. Thinking back to her past Victoria wondered if those obstacles were put in front of her as a test of her mettle. She knew that life was all about being tested and then rising to the occasion. The ideology of self-preservation was preached to her as far back as she could remember. With that in mind Victoria made a conscience effort to maintain that goal as she moved forward. As far as Victoria was concerned life was not always about finding shelter in a storm as much as it was about overcoming the adversities that lay in its wake.

Victoria had given into the fact that she was not always the most logical person on the planet, but she was more than happy with her accomplishments so far.

As Victoria lay awake in bed, she took a moment to digest everything her mother had told her earlier that evening. Victoria felt that after hearing about her father's condition it should have taken more of a toll on her emotions. The news should have been like a cold slap in the face. Yet for some unknown reason it hadn't. In replaying her emotions Victoria found that she took the news rather well. She asked mom all of the right questions but there appeared not to be any sense of urgency behind them. Having time to reflect on her feelings only led to more questions than answers. Perhaps she was trying to stay strong for her mother by not bursting out in a stream of tears. It could also mean that she was learning something about herself. Victoria recalled her own words that this was no time for self-pity. There were countless families that had to deal with hardships, the emotional as well as financial issues. The truth of the matter was that her family was no different. Adversities were all about coming together and reaching out to that one sure thing to make life better in every possible way.

After finishing off her second cup of tea Victoria gave into the fatigue that she was feeling and within ten minutes she was warped into a comfort zone of sleep.

Victoria dreamt of a time when her dad was as mentally sharp as anyone. He appeared to be on top of the world.

It was Christmas morning which fell on a Saturday that year. The night before, Victoria had a difficult time falling asleep. It was well past nine before she finally passed out with dad's help. Dad admitted to having a terrible singing voice. His awful pitch on any Christmas song threatened to send anyone within earshot running for the hills. However, Victoria did not mind her dad's lack of musical skills, simply because as far as she was concerned, he could do anything. Mom on the other hand urged him to let the professionals on the radio handle the holiday singing. On the day after Thanksgiving the radio airwaves were flooded with holiday tunes all the way through the end of December. Each artist put their own spin on the holiday classics from A to Z.

In an effort to show that he would not be bossed around to stop his brand of entertainment, dad promised that he'd pick up where he left off once his throat felt better. Victoria understood that her father could not carry a note but it was a joy to have him around and in such a jovial mood.

Mom and dad had spent time decorating while Victoria did her best to curb her enthusiasm and stay out of their way. Victoria's job each year was to place the star on top of the eight-foot tree after the decorations were set in place. It was the official ringing in of the holiday season at their house. In the past they had always used an artificial tree but this year, dad sprung for the real thing. He said that the smell of fresh evergreen flowing throughout the house added something special to the season. He also said the most important part about having a real tree in the house was keeping it properly watered. There were far too many accidental fires in homes around the country because people forgot to pay attention to this simple detail. It made no sense in having a real tree and not doing the proper things to keep the family safe.

While mom and dad where busy in the kitchen, Victoria had other things on her mind. In the living room Victoria pressed her nose against the large window that looked out onto their street. She could see all the way to Mr. Jenkins' house. It had snowed the night before and the entire neighborhood resembled some of the Christmas cards that hung on their tree as well as the ones in other areas of the house. Victoria noticed that some of the cards looked like grandpa and grandma's house right down to the wisps of smoke that escaped from the chimney.

Victoria and dad built a snowman in front of the house complete with a carrot nose, pieces of coal for the eyes and mouth. Small branches were used for the hands. An old hat and a bright red scarf made it seem alive. Although their hands were almost frozen stiff after the job was completed, it was well worth the effort when they stepped back to admire their work. The front yard was finished off with several white wooden reindeer, star shaped lights that hung from the gutters and pine trees that from Victoria's vantage point below seemed to touch the clouds.

Notwithstanding the beauty of the day and the true meaning of Christmas, Victoria's mind was focused on the presents beneath the tree. A rainbow of treasures to be had Victoria felt, and she could not wait to attack any one that held her name.

Just before the holiday break Victoria recalled how her teacher took the entire class to the mall where the assignment for the day was to purchase a gift for their parents or guardian. The hardest part of the assignment as far as Victoria was concerned called for wrapping the presents. However with a large measure of assistance, the class did a pretty good job. Victoria bought a sweater for her mother and a hat for her father. Victoria even had fun designing the Christmas card. Although the words were written in her childish scrawl she was pleased with the effort. The card was placed on its own branch of the tree just above their presents.

"When can we open the gifts?" Victoria asked as she burst into the kitchen. The tone of her voice revealed the inner excitement that raced through her small frame.

Even at her young age it was difficult for Victoria to contain her emotions. It really didn't matter if she were angry or happy about a particular situation. The way she felt was always pasted on her face and in the sound of her voice. She was told her on more than one occasion that her emotions would either get her into a world of trouble or it would be the fuel which opened the doors to success.

"Presents?" Gayle responded as if there was nothing under the tree worth mentioning.

"Is that the only thing your little mind can think about?" There was a stern yet playful tone in her voice.

"Uh oh," Wesley said as he turned his gaze in Victoria's direction. "You've done it now."

"You hush yourself," Gayle ordered.

"This is girl stuff between mother and daughter. We'll have breakfast first, church second and then we'll open our presents," Gayle said in an ordered fashion.

"But we went to church last night," Victoria mildly protested.

At the sound of his daughter's response, Wesley eased himself out of his chair and turned toward the living room as if he'd forgotten something. He thought about the warning he had given Victoria about that mouth of hers and the trouble it could visit upon her. Wesley knew that when it came to church services Gayle did not play around.

"That's okay honey," Gayle began.

"I have it on good authority that the Lord won't mind the company." Gayle kissed both of Victoria's cheeks.

Although Victoria was not particularly satisfied with the answer, she was smart enough to know when to fight her battles and when to recognize when the war was over. Her dad's words also played a large part in her decision.

Christmas dinner was filled with family members from near and far. There were aunts and uncles that Victoria hadn't seen in years. Aunt Janice was always good for a special gift or two. It didn't matter if it were her birthday or a reward for doing well in school, she always came through with something great. Beside her mom and dad Aunt Janice was her favorite relative.

Uncle Theo did his usual thing after dinner. He entertained himself by lounging on the couch and watching parts of every ballgame on television. Last month he went skiing and broke his right leg. Although the doctors had done a masterful job in getting him back on his feet, the procedure left him with a noticeable limp. While he had to use a cane to get around comfortably Uncle Theo was upbeat about the whole affair as he told the story of his recovery. He especially missed being on the mountains and competing in the cross-country races.

"At least my bum leg hasn't forced me to cut down on ballroom dancing," he joked.

"But maybe I should have taken up something less risky like race car driving. I hear the Indy 500 is looking for new blood." Uncle Theo's face turned beet red as he laughed so hard, he momentarily lost his breath.

Uncle Theo was in his mid-thirties and as far as Victoria could tell he seemed much too old for skiing or racing cars for that matter. She believed that to be true no matter how many times her dad said that you were only as young as you felt. That kind of logic Victoria couldn't understand. In her world if you were old then you were old and that was the end of it. But again, Victoria exercised better judgment and kept her thoughts locked away.

Months later Victoria had her heart set on learning how to ride a bicycle. Wesley bought Victoria a bike as part of her reward for doing well in school.

Gayle and Wesley thought back on their youthful days and realized that school as it stood now was nothing like when they were Victoria's age. It was light years away judging by the technological advances and the pressures society placed on young people nowadays. Of course, life was much simpler then and the choices were limited once they reached early adulthood. There was school, homework and chores to be completed. Wesley remembered that on Saturday afternoons he was allowed to play outside but it wasn't until was at least twelve years old that he could leave the block for more than an hour. At fifteen, he could to go to the park and shoot baskets with his friends David, Ralph and Joseph.

Wesley recalled that the four of them were like brothers. If you saw one of them in the neighborhood it was more than likely that you'd run into the other three within the next few minutes. Wesley was three months older than the other guys and for the most part he acted as the leader of the group. Not that he abused the role that was thrust on him it was just the way things worked back then.

When they were old enough to go to parties Wesley and David took on new roles among the group. They were the Casanovas of the neighborhood. It was a role that they took pride in and played it extremely well. Wesley was a little more of a charmer than David and most of the girls flocked to him. Wesley was the best athlete in his class and he led his High School to several divisional championships. Wesley and his friends lived their lives as virtual kings of the neighborhood. There were also special perks and favors afforded to them especially on game nights. Mr. Russo would always throw in an extra slice of pizza at no charge. Life back then was simple and rewarding at the same time.

It was a Saturday afternoon and Victoria was up bright and early. She wiped the sleep from her eyes, washed up and got dressed. She was ready to begin the day well before nine o'clock.

Victoria had no sense of time. In her small-minded world, a promise was a promise. Victoria had slept with her pink and white Road Tracer helmet at the foot of her bed. Victoria had everything she would need to ensure her safety including wrist guards and knee pads. Victoria mildly protested at her dad's condition that she have training wheels attached to her bicycle before they started out. Victoria complained that training wheels were for kids and rookies. Victoria refused to recognize that she was a member of both groups and Wesley took the time to remind her of that fact. With some measure of resignation Victoria acknowledged her membership in the groups and mounted the bicycle in spite of her unsteady frame.

Wesley held the back of the bicycle while Victoria began to peddle. She had trouble keeping the handle bars directly in front of her no matter how tightly she held on. They turned to the left, then to the right and back again.

"Try and keep the handle bars in front of you," Wesley said with encouragement. Victoria tightened her grip hoping that would do the trick. However, she failed miserably and almost toppled over taking Wesley down with her.

"I'll never learn how to ride that stupid thing," Victoria lamented in total resignation. Her level of frustration rose and she was almost on the verge of tears.

"All it takes is a little more practice honey," Wesley said. He wanted to keep his comments upbeat for Victoria's sake. Although she was slightly undersized for the bike there was no reason to think that she couldn't master the task if she stuck to it. Victoria had never intentionally given up on anything in her young life and this was not the time to do so.

Victoria was standing on the sidewalk looking down at the bicycle as if it were some sort of mechanical beast that sneered at her in mocking fashion. Its features changed right before her eyes. The spokes which adorned the wheels were like teeth ready to tear through flesh and bone if someone touched it again.

"Maybe I don't want to learn how to ride that stupid thing after all," Victoria said with a fair amount of conviction in her voice.

"Do you really want to give up now?" Wesley asked knowing that Vicky really didn't mean what she said.

"C'mon Vicky, I know you really don't mean that. Let's give it another try. I know that you can do it," Wesley said.

After a few moments of hesitation Victoria mounted the bicycle once again. This time there was a look of determination on her face. As before Wesley held on to the back of the bike as Victoria's small feet worked the peddles. She had control of the monster as she referred to the bicycle moments ago.

"Don't go to fast or you might lose control," Wesley cautioned. Without Victoria realizing it Wesley let go of the seat and Victoria was on her own.

"Take it nice and easy and everything will be just fine. Concentrate on keeping the handle bars in front of you like I said before. Make believe that you're trying to walk a straight line on the road," Wesley suggested.

For the first fifty feet or so Victoria had it. She was actually riding without making any mistakes. The fear of falling seemed as if it never existed. Her heart began beating faster with the excitement she was feeling inside.

"Keep it up Vicky," Wesley shouted with delight.

"You're doing it!"

For a split-second Victoria felt slightly unsure at the idea that she was actually controlling the bike. But she would not let that stop her. As she continued down the sidewalk Victoria momentarily lost control of the bike. But she corrected her mistake like the champion she knew she could be. In her mind she was participating in a world class motor cross event as a seasoned veteran.

Victoria was almost at the end of the block which was considered new territory. She stopped the bike and turned toward her father and in an excited voice she called back to him.

"Can I keep going daddy?" she squealed.

Wesley thought carefully before responding to the request.

"Okay. But just remember Rome wasn't built in a day and there are still a few things that you have to work on. Using the brakes and watching out for people on the sidewalk are just as important as learning how to ride," Wesley cautioned.

Victoria flashed the okay sign. Yet in her mind she felt that people should watch out for her. After all, she was the professional. At least for the time being.

"You can go one more block then turn around. I think I've created a monster here," Wesley called out in a joking manner. This was a phrase that he used when referring to Vicky and her unbridled spirit. He was unsure if he'd ever let it go even into her adult life. Only time would tell.

Wesley watched as Victoria peddled further and further away. Ten feet, twenty feet, thirty feet. Good God he thought if only Gayle could see her daughter now.

As Victoria took off down the block Wesley saw two things, Victoria's feet and the back of her head. He marveled at how she had grown over the years. Wesley recalled how he'd wished Victoria would stay young forever. He wondered how he would handle the thought of her growing up and forgetting about him or not seeking his counsel when it came to life's problems. Although Wesley knew that he would have to let her go someday he was powerless to slow the hands of time. He was not emotionally ready to give up being everything that she needed as her father and protector. Wesley imagined that most parents felt that way about their children when they were young, but that would never cushion the harsh blow that reality had in store for them.

Wesley tried to discuss this with Gayle. However, she responded by accusing him of being an over protective father. But in his mind, this was a label that he wore proudly and never took Gayle's comment as an insult.

Wesley understood that he would have to let Vicky go out into the world and discover things on her own.

Wesley watched as Victoria had gone far enough before he called out for her to come back. Wesley realized that this was going to be a day to remember for the rest of his life and the thought brought a wide smile to his face. In the grand scheme of things past and present the task of teaching your child how to ride a bicycle may not seem important. But emotionally speaking, to Wesley it was equal to finding the mystery of life itself. There was a sense of accomplishment for the child and a sense of pride for the teacher.

By the time Thursday morning rolled in Sharon realized that she hadn't seen Victoria at all. Although she was busy with her own problems there was always some reason or another that their paths would cross. Sharon checked the time. At a quarter past nine Victoria had to be in her office or at least somewhere in the building. She may even be in the cafeteria buying a cup of coffee and a cream cheese bagel. This was something they had done together on countless mornings after arriving for work and certainly before going their separate ways.

Sharon decided to take matters in her own hands and find Victoria before beginning her day. During her search Sharon wondered if Victoria spoke to her mother and patched things up concerning her father. It was extremely important that mother and daughter were on the same page. Although Sharon had known Victoria for quite a while a part of her wondered if she'd over stepped her bounds when voicing an opinion. Perhaps she had no right in lecturing Victoria on what to do when it came to her family. At times the territorial landscape between events that occurred at work and life outside of the office can be fragile and dangerous if not traveled carefully. While Victoria never gave any indication that she had gone too far but it was something that Sharon had to seriously consider. She remembered making that mistake once before. It happened years ago but it was something that she would never forget.

Heather was one of her oldest and closest friends in high school. Sharon was the new kid on the block, a freshman and Heather was a year ahead. It didn't take long for Sharon to see that even the juniors and seniors respected Heather. This was not the way any school's hierarchy usually worked. The upper classmen had no problem with including Heather in activities that any other freshman or sophomore would give their eye-teeth to be a part of on any day of the week.

Sharon discovered that Heather had a free spirited and liberal personality. However, she didn't like people telling her what to do when her mind was made up. Sharon recalled a time when their conversation turned personal. The issue involved Heather's relationship with a guy named Derrick. The mention of his name brought feelings of anger and distrust to Sharon. In a few simple words he was no good for her best friend.

Her advice that Heather stop seeing Derrick didn't go over as well as she would have liked. For the first time Sharon learned that there were boundaries between being friends and telling them the truth. In its current use of the word, Derrick was a dog in every way possible. He sniffed around and sexually growled at any woman who passed within his imagined domain. Which in his case was any place under the sun.

Sharon discovered that Derrick was seeing two other girls while professing his love for Heather. Sharon knew that her information was legitimate and not an allegation born from unfounded gossip. Sharon debated long and hard on whether she should tell Heather the truth about Derrick or keep the information under lock and key. Sharon realized that in matters of the heart good advice sometimes fell on deaf ears. But Sharon could not live with the fact that her friend was being taken advantage of by someone who failed to possess a moral compass or a natural sense of right and wrong.

Heather revealed that being with Derrick was like dating Dr. Jeckel, Mr. Hyde and Valentino all rolled into a single individual. The term "*monsters and lovers*" surfaced when she thought about Derrick. Yet no matter how bad things had become Heather confessed to being in love with him. Perhaps he possessed that bad boy image Heather had been warned about before she began dating. Derrick was handsome in every way imaginable. His light green eyes set against his caramel-colored skin tone were mesmerizing. Derrick's look pulled Heather in as if she had no will of her own. However, in spite of his God-given looks, Sharon saw something different. Just as intoxicating as he looked on the outside, he was equally flawed on the inside.

Sharon always listened closely to Heather's words when it came to Derrick and for the most part, she remained silent. But this time she couldn't hold back. By the time she found the strength to bring the truth about Derrick to the surface she quickly found out why the more intelligent thing to do was to keep her mouth shut. After telling Heather about the *"real"* Derrick and his self-serving ways, Heather verbally attacked with the speed and the deadly intent of a startled viper. She accused Sharon of being jealous. Heather painted Sharon as someone who didn't have a love life of her own and was attempting to destroy the joy and happiness that she had found. Sharon recalled how she tried to defend herself against Heather's accusations but nothing seemed to assuage the situation. As much as she tried to reason with Heather the more enflamed things had become.

That was a life time ago and going forward she and Heather have never spoken to each other again. The exchanging of birthday and holiday cards became a thing of the past. Sharon realized that there was no going back to the way things used to be between them. The relationship was for all intents and purposes dead and buried.

Sharon never found out whether the veil over Heather's eyes were lifted and she came to see that Derrick was playing her for a fool. Sharon understood that she couldn't live Heather's life for her. However, the job of a true friend was to provide solid advice and be there in a time of need. But in this case, it hadn't worked out that way. As ugly as reality can be, on its own the truth can be a vicious bitch with sharp teeth and claws to match.

In other words, merciless.

As the elevator steadily climbed the enclosed shaft, Sharon wondered if she was not making the same mistake when it came to giving advice to a friend. Although she valued Victoria's friendship and would never do anything to put that in jeopardy, she also had to consider not stepping into a place where she may not necessarily be wanted. That being said, Victoria never seemed to be that stubborn where she would dismiss good advice. But if things failed to go as planned Sharon knew that she would obey the warning signs and engage in a hasty retreat before their friendship crashed and burned.

Victoria didn't feel like working today. No matter how much she tried to focus on a particular project her thoughts reverted back to her parents. The truth of the matter was that Victoria wanted to be left alone. No visitors or phone calls. Victoria didn't want anything to soil the cloak of solitude that she had draped around her shoulders. If anyone showed up looking for any kind of conversation, she would give them "*the bum's rush*" and resort back to the deserted island she created in her mind.

The morning continued as if Victoria was living out someone else's life while being trapped in her own body. It was difficult for her to understand what she was feeling. There was never a time when she was at work where she failed to give it her all. The lack of focus was in direct conflict with her usual sense of efficiency and enthusiasm. The person sitting behind the desk was nothing like the Victoria of several weeks ago. Yet here she was trapped with no escape to be found.

Victoria absently leafed through a small stack of documents on her desk hoping there was some urgent message that would alter her current state of being. However, she found nothing that would help disperse the dark cloud of depression that hung over her.

Just as Victoria completed the thought there was a knock on the door and Sharon entered. Little did Sharon know at the time that she was the breath of fresh air that Victoria needed. Victoria offered Sharon a cup of coffee before she took a seat in front of Victoria's desk.

They began talking about anything and everything that came to mind. Victoria spoke about the latest news concerning her father.

"How much does Jasmine know about your dad and has she began to ask questions?" Sharon put forward.

"Jasmine's a pretty smart kid. She knows there's something different about her grandfather but she doesn't fully understand what it is. At least not yet and to be honest, I'm not sure how to tell her," Victoria confessed.

"What about relatives?" Sharon asked.

"Have you or your mother opened up to them about your dad's condition? It's important because you wouldn't want anyone to be caught by surprise. Believe me, anger won't begin to tell the whole story," Sharon offered.

Victoria revealed that her mother had spoken to their relatives near and far based on the very same reasons Sharon just mentioned.

Sharon took a sip from her cup of coffee before she began speaking again. This time she turned the conversation to another important issue. Namely Victoria's personal wellbeing.

"Since it looks as if you're on the road to recovery I think it's time you started dating. In my case it was almost two years before I even considered romance. But you know once I put my mind to it, I realized that I made the right decision to get back out there. I found out that life wasn't as bad as I thought," Sharon revealed obviously feeling good about her decision.

Victoria looked long and hard at Sharon. Although she was not a trained psychologist Sharon made a pretty good impression of one at the moment. From where Victoria sat perhaps Sharon was right in her assessment. Shoring up the romantic side of her life may need some attention. At the very least a peek inside. Victoria humorously made the decision not to confess any of her other shortcomings in the area of romance.

A smile of hope appeared on Victoria's face before she responded to Sharon's suggestion.

"Did you have someone special in mind?" Victoria asked kind of hoping that Sharon was joking.

Having Sharon, her mother or anyone else for that matter attempt to fix her up was not an option Victoria was willing to consider. If love were to come around again it would be on her terms. Blind dates were usually a disaster. In her humble opinion there were too many unknown variables to consider before going down that rabbit hole. Victoria reasoned that she had enough on her plate right now. Between dad, mom and Jasmine, getting involved in a romantic relationship was simply out of the question.

"Well since you asked my dear. There's this really attractive guy on the twenty-third floor. Word is he's single, loves kids and drives a Jag," Sharon announced as if she were the man's press agent.

Victoria snapped the thumb and middle finger of her right hand in mock disappointment.

"Damn Sharon, you had me until you mentioned his car. You see I've made it a hard and fast rule to only go out with guys that drive American."

"Funny. Very funny," Sharon dryly responded.

Victoria and Sharon talked for another hour before they both decided that being at work paid the bills and they would continue this conversation at some other point in time. Victoria felt so much better after talking with Sharon and for the moment she was back to her old self. She picked up the telephone on the second ring and was ready to tackle anything that might be thrown her way.

Friday evening could not have come soon enough. Victoria was looking forward to relaxing after she got Jasmine cleaned up and ready for bed. A stress-free evening was just what the doctor ordered.

"Mom when are we going to see grandma and grandpa again?" Jasmine asked. Her voice was high pitched and laden with excitement.

"I haven't seen them since my birthday," Jasmine added.

In an instant there were a thousand thoughts running around inside Victoria's head. God forgive her but she certainly didn't want to tell Jasmine the truth about her grandfather. It was better that the facts should be hidden from her as long as possible.

"I know honey. Grandma and grandpa have been very busy the last couple of weeks. They're doing some renovations on their house so that's taking up a lot of their free time," Victoria said.

Truth.

"About a month ago grandpa had a roofing contractor come over and examine the discoloration caused by the changing seasons. Maybe we can go over there this weekend," Victoria said.

Victoria had spent a lifetime shielding Jasmine from the worst that life had to offer. Her shroud of protection extended to the kind of music Jasmine listened to, her choice of clothing and her time surfing the internet. Although Jasmine did not always agree with her decision, she never put up much of an argument.

For a better part of the morning Gayle passed the time wandering aimlessly through the entire house. She adjusted the framed pictures around the living room three or four times without actually being aware of what she was doing. It was obvious that she was frustrated and worried at the same time. Gayle wiped down the bookshelves in the den with the same robotic fashion. Although she hated the task of dusting it kept her mind off thinking about Wesley and the argument they got into last night. Of course, it was over something silly and Gayle would be hard pressed to remember exactly what started the disagreement that became so heated. It was like that old saying she recalled which went something like this *Bad news always seems to travel faster than good news can get its pants on.* In other words, the worst part of any situation always seems to arrive ahead of time.

Suddenly the reason for their heated exchange popped into Gayle's mind. It was like one of those times where you're trying to remember the name of a song. You were taxing your memory all day but nothing happened. Then in a flash of total recall it came to you.

Wesley became upset because she put black satin sheets on the bed with olive green pillow cases. Wesley didn't like the color scheme feeling that the combination screamed military. Army in his opinion. Wesley was so angry that he couldn't remember where he left his bathrobe. He blamed her for that too.

Gayle prayed that Wesley's mood had changed for the better since he had a doctor's appointment this afternoon. Gayle had planned on leaving early but she was not sure how long it would take Wesley to get himself together. There was a time when he would jump out of bed and into his clothes in no time flat. Then he would complain that she was taking too much time getting ready. But Gayle quickly realized just how much things had changed and now the shoe was on the other foot so to speak. When Gayle peeked into their bathroom, she saw Wesley standing in front of the mirror fully dressed and adjusting his tie and the collar of his shirt.

"Well I'll be," Gayle said in a mocking fashion.

"The last time I checked you were sleeping like a baby."

"I figured we'd better get to the doctor's office a little early. You know how I hate waiting around. Remember the last time? The appointment was scheduled for eleven- thirty, but we didn't get to see the doctor until well past twelve," Wesley lamented.

"True. But Dr. McCain was backed up that day so our late arrival really didn't matter that much," Gayle said.

"All right I'll give you that," Wesley responded as he looked in the mirror and ran his fingers over his freshly shaved chin.

"I don't know about you but the last thing I want to do is spend a gorgeous day in a doctor's office waiting to be seen. It's just as bad as being at the DMV waiting for your number to show up on that stupid digital screen," Wesley complained.

There was a sense of frustration in Wesley's voice that Gayle found refreshing. It was good to see him this feisty and worked up about something besides complaining for complaining's sake.

"All right settle down mister," Gayle offered in response to her husband's tirade.

"Give me ten minutes and I'll be ready. I want to make sure that I can put my hands on my medical and insurance cards. Sound good to you?" Wesley playfully asked.

True to form in ten minutes husband and wife were out the door locked arm in arm. The car service that Gayle called for met them in their driveway.

As much as Victoria attempted to concentrate on the job, she had trouble dismissing her last conversation with Sharon. The thought of getting back into the dating scene had its pitfalls but at the same time there was something attractive about the idea. Victoria conceded to Sharon's description. Thomas was an attractive man.

Thomas worked in the technology department and the word around said that he was a genius when it came to computer programing and troubleshooting. It was said that he could be making twice as much money if he chose to put his skills on the market. Victoria jokingly wished that she had that option.

Romantic probabilities aside Victoria was unsure if she really wanted take the time to get to know Thomas on a personal level. Suppose he had irreversible hang-ups that no one knew about? Suppose he was an axe murderer wanted throughout the continental United States? Suppose he was not into successful black women? Suppose he was not into black women at all? Suppose he was gay? Suppose he had mother issues?

In a moment of clarity Victoria realized that she was fishing for any excuse not to try her hand at romance. But then if Sharon mentioned him as a possibility, then he must be okay.

Right?

The issue Victoria faced was in opening the lines of communication that did not involve work? Victoria knew she was nothing like Carole who would approach Thomas and boldly ask if he would like to have lunch and then take it from there. Victoria knew that was not her style.

Being bold and straightforward was a useful character trait when it came to business but that brand of bravado never spilled over into her personal life. Perhaps she was simply a ball of nerves. As much as Victoria tried to convince herself that it was something else, she knew the truth without having to place her hand on a bible.

For the moment Victoria was filled with a self-doubt that she hadn't experienced in quite a while. Victoria wondered if she had anything to bring to the table when it came to romance. If it didn't involve facts, figures and charts Victoria considered herself a lost cause. In the past she had always been confident and self-assured in the direction life was taking her and if anything got in her way, she would knock it over. Full speed ahead was her motto as she moved up the corporate ladder. At one point she was labeled as being cold and callous. However, Victoria would counter those criticisms as her being focused and determined. It was not a matter of her seeking anyone's approval. It was important that everyone take her seriously when it came to the level of drive and commitment she possessed.

Just as Victoria realized this was no time to analyze her shortcomings the telephone came to life and mercifully, she was returned to her world of facts, figures and charts.

In other words, her comfort zone.

Victoria listened to Katherine's voice on the other end of the phone. Her head slowly bobbed up and down in acknowledgement as she scribbled notes on the yellow legal pad in front of her.

Halfway through the conversation Victoria's jaw tightened which was a sure sign that the news was like a punch in the stomach. In an effort to remain as calm as possible Victoria mentally told herself that she could handle the problem. After the call Victoria leaned as far back in her chair as it would allow before possibly tipping over. Apparently, someone had screwed up and deleted the entire financial portfolio related to their latest client. Victoria felt as if a fifty-pound weight had been tied to her ankle as she was on the last leg of a ten-mile race. It had taken Victoria and her team months to put that information together and present it to the board.

Victoria asked if any of the information could be retrieved. She was told there was a possibility that some of it may have been automatically saved on a backup system. But Victoria took note of Katherine's tone which said that the files were likely lost for good. But there was always hope. Katherine would never openly admit defeat being the optimist that everyone knew her to be. Victoria realized that she would probably feel the same way if she were in Katherine's shoes. In business it was always better to look on the bright side in the face of any disaster.

Victoria and everyone involved with the project had two days to resolve the setback. The best way to keep the problem under control was to keep the bad news to a minimum. Her job was to remain positive and focused knowing that somehow, they would get through this crisis.

During the drive to Dr. McCain's office Gayle noticed that Wesley barely said a word. Whenever she attempted to engage him in any meaningful conversation Wesley's responses were short or downright choppy at best. A "Yes," here, a "Maybe," there. Once in a while he would become a full-blown chatter box and respond with something like "I know you'll make the right decision." Gayle didn't want to make a big deal over her husband's sudden lack of communication and pestering him about it would certainly lead to an argument which was the last thing she wanted.

In an effort to keep her mind occupied Gayle pulled out a pamphlet from her bag which seemed to contain just about anything that one could imagine. She began to leaf through the pages until an article caught her attention. It recommended that seniors look for ways to lower the costs of their medication. They should also begin a low impact exercise routine and change their diet. Gayle thought about her husband and how badly he might react to the suggestion.

As the car pulled into the parking lot of the doctor's office Wesley came to life.

"Finally," he said in an exasperated tone while reaching for his wallet to pay the twenty-dollar fare which included a three-dollar tip.

Wesley came around to Gayle's side and helped her out of the car. At least that part of his memory was still intact Gayle thought.

"Maybe when this is all over, we can go get something to eat," Wesley said.

"As long as you're buying," Gayle responded with a wide smile pasted on her face.

After they entered the waiting area Wesley took a mental count of the room.

Seven.

Wesley took a seat while Gayle added his name to the sign in sheet. The receptionist behind the desk was an attractive young lady who stopped what she was doing and asked which doctor they were here to see and the time of their appointment. Gayle felt that she had similar facial features to her daughter. A caramel-colored skin tone and the cutest dimples. However, the similarities pretty much ended there. The receptionist had on these oversized hoops that dangled from her ear lobes. They danced back and forth and from side to side with the movement of her head. As far as Gayle could see they were a distraction and took away from her outward natural beauty.

Gayle responded that her husband was here to see Dr. McCain and the appointment was set for one o'clock.

"You're not a new patient, are you?" she asked.

"No, my husband has been a patient of his for quite a while," Gayle responded.

"Okay. We're updating our patient profiles so would you mind having your husband fill out this questionnaire?" she asked.

As the receptionist raised her arm to hand over the clipboard, Gayle noticed that her right forearm bore floral patterned tattoos of varying shapes and size. Gayle couldn't imagine why anyone would defile them self in such a manner. The bible said that the body was a temple and

Gayle believed that to treat it in such a way was being disrespectful to its creator. Nonetheless Gayle did her best to mask the displeasure she felt inside and smiled as she took the clipboard from the receptionist.

Gayle took a seat on her husband's left side. He was lost in a sports magazine and completely unaware of her presence. That changed when Wesley expressed his opinion on the article.

The subject was professional football.

"Look at this. They pay these guys a boat load of money to play ball and you'd think they might win a game or two along the way," Wesley complained.

Although his words were probably true Gayle wished that Wesley would lower his voice just a bit. She was fairly certain that everyone in the waiting area did not need or want to hear his opinion. Undoubtedly there were more important things on their mind considering their current location.

Gayle gave him a slight nudge protesting the volume of his voice. Wesley toned it down but he still complained about the fact that to many ballplayers nowadays were being coddled and were overpaid.

Gayle scanned the area where they were seated. Her eyes locked on a gentleman seemingly close to Wesley's age seated directly across from her. The expression on his face and the nodding of his head said that he agreed with her husband's opinion, yet he kept the thought to himself.

Almost a half an hour later Wesley's name was called and a young woman in a pale blue uniform ushered them into one of the examination rooms. The physician's assistant informed them that Dr. McCain would be with them after he finished up with another patient.

"In the meantime, I'm going to check your vitals. I'll start with your weight," she said.

Wesley removed his jacket and shoes. Without actually being aware of it he pulled in his stomach just as both feet hit the platform of the scale. Wesley stared straight ahead focusing his attention on a poster of the inner human body on the wall.

Out of concern regarding his weight Wesley took a peek at the large square metal peg that hung on the horizontal arm of the scale. The assistant slid the metal block from the left to the right. As she was about to reach the two hundred-pound range Wesley cleared his throat as a sign of protest. The assistant paid no attention and proceeded to move the large and smaller weights back to the left in an effort to balance the arm.

There was a sign of relief on Wesley's face when she announced his weight at one hundred-seventy-three pounds. Wesley was afraid that he was going to top out at over two hundred pounds based of the way he'd been eating over the last month. Thankfully that was not the case.

"It's a good thing you took your shoes off," Gayle playfully commented.

"You'd be surprised at the number of people who will not get on the scale without taking off their footwear. The number won't change from the time you enter until the time you leave because the scale isn't going to lie," the assistant said in a matter-of-fact tone.

Gayle carefully watched her husband's movement when the assistant requested that he move to the examination table. The assistant set up the machine to begin the process of checking Wesley's blood pressure. After a few minutes had passed she announced that he was well within the acceptable range. After checking Wesley's breathing, she made a few notations in his file. Then finally it was a matter of drawing blood. This was the part of the examination that Wesley hated the most.

The assistant drew two vials worth.

"That's all for now. The doctor should be in shortly," she said before leaving the room.

Five minutes later Dr. McCain entered. He thumbed through Wesley's file before speaking.

"I see you've taken off a few pounds since your last check up," the doctor said with a smile of approval registered on his face.

Wesley responded in kind.

"While that's definitely something to be proud of but you still have to be careful with your body. As I mentioned the last time we have to watch your cholesterol level. The good as well as the bad," he added.

Dr. McCain mentioned that he would have the results of the blood work in a day or so and would call Wesley with the results. He asked if Wesley needed any refills for his medications. Wesley thought for a moment before responding that he was fine. Gayle nodded in the doctor's direction as confirmation to her husband's response.

"Well, if there's nothing else, I'd say you're in pretty good shape. Are there any concerns or questions you may have?" the doctor asked.

Gayle was standing next to her husband's right side. There was a look of concern on her face that she tried to hide. She looked in the doctor's direction and asked whether a blood test can detect signs of memory loss. The question spilled out of her mouth before she could pull it back.

"Is there someone in particular that you're worried about?" the doctor asked. He did his best not to look in Wesley's direction.

Gayle hated herself when she lied and said that she was simply curious after watching a medical program on television a few days ago.

The doctor said that although he was not a neurologist, physicians can have blood drawn and specifically test for signs of mental depreciation. There have been some success in identifying patients with early onset dementia through MRI screening. Also, an MRI can find a level of brain tissue loss which can detect the difference between Alzheimer's disease and frontotemporal dementia.

"However, a CT is the most common type of brain scan in order to identify the disease. If you need more information, I can put out a few feelers," the doctor offered.

"No thank you. That won't be necessary" Gayle quickly responded. "I was just curious," she added.

Wesley stepped away from the doctor and looked in his wife's direction. His expression said that he was less than pleased with Gayle's inquiry and her bringing up the subject in the first place. He knew very well that she was referring to him and he didn't like it at all. Perhaps the doctor knew as well what she was up too.

Before leaving the examination room the doctor reminded Wesley to see the receptionist and schedule his next appointment.

Wesley began to get dressed and although he didn't verbalize his feelings everything about his movements said that he was glad to be leaving. In spite of the fact that Wesley bragged about maintaining his weight he could go for something inexpensive yet satisfying. If Gayle gave him any crap about it, he would tell her to take it up with the doctor and hopefully that would be the end of it.

One of the best things about New York that made it worthwhile was the fact that you could find anything your heart desired at any time of the day or night. In Wesley's opinion New York was the culinary capital of the world and there was no other city that could compete with such a prodigious title. The problem was deciding what and where he wanted to eat. Gayle would likely suggest a salad but he wanted something with a little more kick. It was too early in the day for a three-course meal but Wesley wanted something to cure his hunger pains. Gayle suggested that they try the same restaurant they went to after their last appointment.

"You remember," Gayle began.

"The one on Fifty-Third Street and Second Avenue. At least we can be sure that the food is fresh," Gayle remarked.

Wesley nodded in agreement at his wife's suggestion while rubbing the palms of his hands together. He recalled giving the restaurant a three-star rating.

"I have no problem with that," Wesley said as if visions of his last meal were about to be laid out in front of him.

"Then its Valencio's," Gayle said.

Deciding not to call for a car service, they were lucky to get the first empty taxi that came their way before it was snatched up by someone else.

As Wesley and Gayle entered the restaurant sounds of plates clanging against one another and meal orders being placed filled the air. Waiters briskly moved from one side of the dining area to the other carrying plates laden with food. The scent of steaks being grilled and other consumable delights assaulted their senses.

The reason for the smile on Wesley's face was clearly obvious.

"Table for two?" the hostess asked.

"Yes indeed," Wesley eagerly responded.

Wesley and Gayle were escorted to a row of booths near the oversized windows giving them an unobstructed view of the street.

After a few moments had passed a waiter appeared carrying two glasses of iced water and a pair of menus that were tucked securely between his left ribcage and forearm. Wesley guessed that the man must have been having a pretty good day judging by the smile on his face as he approached. He was dressed in a white shirt, a bow tie, black vest and pants. He walked with a slight yet noticeable limp. With a Latin accent he bid them good afternoon and asked if they would like something to drink besides water.

Gale requested a cup of tea and Wesley coffee.

The waiter handed Gayle a menu before giving one to Wesley. He asked if they would like to hear the specials of the day. Husband and wife responded that they would. Each listened attentively as the waiter ran through a list of six possible selections featuring beef, fish, lamb, chicken, pork and vegetable. Each dish appeared more delectable than the prior recommendation.

"Take your time and I'll be back to take your orders," the waiter said. He bowed slightly before turning away.

Gayle closely watched as Wesley took a long sip of his cup of coffee as if he were consuming a rare liquid treat.

"You do realize that will be your third cup of the day?" Gayle asked in a concerned manner.

"Are you sure that you really want to do that to yourself?" she added.

Wesley's face contorted as if attempting to solve a complex equation before he responded to his wife's question or her verbal jab as he took it.

"I simply want to compare it to the pot I made this morning. I didn't think anyone could make a better cup of coffee," Wesley offered.

"I've tasted your coffee and believe me it's nothing to brag about," Gayle said with a smile.

Without further thought of his wife's comment, Wesley turned his attention to the menu in his hands. His eyes scanned the pages and within a few moments Wesley made his choice.

As promised the waiter returned in short order. He jotted down their meal requests as if he were trained in the skill of dictation.

"Very good choices," the waiter commented before he turned away once again.

Wesley watched as the man pushed his way through two swinging steel doors and disappeared.

"I wonder if we'll see Victoria today? "Gayle asked. "I spoke with her the day before yesterday and she said that if time allowed, she'd bring Jasmine over for a visit."

A look of surprise appeared on Wesley's face.

"I didn't know you spoke with her. What time was that?" he asked.

"It was some time after eight. Jasmine had gone to bed already so we had time to chat. It was mostly girl talk. Nothing you'd be interested in," Gayle said.

Wesley said nothing in response thinking Gayle was probably right. Instead, he poked at the steak and the accompanying garlic mashed potato on his plate. He pushed the broccoli aside treating it as a distant cousin.

Out of the blue Wesley's attention was drawn to the chatter coming from a family seated across from them. Their conversation could be heard from here to Brooklyn. The young girl's father seemed to be reprimanding her about being out past curfew. His tone was bathed in anger as he spoke. The man's hands were slightly raised and they cut through the air as a matter of emphasis. The armpits of his light blue shirt were soaked. There were visible beads of perspiration dotting his forehead. He reminded his daughter that even though she was growing up that as long as she lived under his roof there were rules she had to obey.

His wife remained silent. She passed the time during the lecture by shoving food into her mouth.

She was a smallish thin boned woman who obviously did not get out much judging by her pale features. Black roots were visible through her badly dyed blonde hair and in Gayle's opinion the woman had on too much lipstick. The ghastly red color smeared across her lips appeared to have been applied by a child playing dress up. Or worse yet an adult without the gift of sight.

Gayle took a look at the young girl's expression as her father continued his tirade. Her face appeared to say "Yeah right dad. Whatever." Her eyes rolled toward the back of her head and Gayle could swear she heard the girl suck her teeth in response to her father's words.

Also seated at the booth was a young boy who couldn't have been more than two years old. He appeared to be in a world of his own as he worked on the bowl of ice cream in front of him. By the mess he was making Gayle could see that chocolate was his favorite flavor.

At the sight of his face the boy's mother lashed out.

"What do you think they make napkins for?" she asked while attempting to clean the child's face.

As far as Gayle could see the woman's concern should have been focused on the conversation between father and daughter regarding her obvious disrespect.

Her son was simply enjoying himself and causing no real harm. The worst thing he could have done was to soil his pants every now and again. Harmless stuff in the grand scheme of things one would think. Gayle imagined that any mishap would more than likely set off a barrage of verbal abuse directed at the child.

After a few more comments from her disapproving father, the young girl who the man identified as Samantha spoke for the first time in her defense.

"I'm almost seventeen and I don't see the big deal with coming home a little last past your curfew." Her tone was argumentative and boarded on defiance. Judging by her attitude it was clear that this was not the first time she violated the rules set down by her parents.

Teenagers usually build up to the level of bravado now on display when it came to defying their parents. Samantha felt extremely comfortable and ready to defend the rights she believed she had in spite of the fact that in the eyes of the law she was still a minor.

Finally, Samantha's mother found her voice and directed her comments at her daughter.

"Samantha that's no way to speak to your father. You had better understand and get it through your head that it's your dad's house and he's in charge."

At hearing those words, a look of pleasure appeared on the man's face. He liked the fact that although he wasn't the top dog at work, at home he was the law. His wife also towed the line when it came to his rules. There were certain things that she was supposed have done and ready by the time her husband got home. Namely dinner, beer and sex whether she liked it or not.

"But don't I have a life too?" Samantha asked. This time her tone was slightly more civil and less challenging. Yet she still wanted to get her point across that she didn't agree with her father. Samantha especially didn't like the fact that her father for all intents and purposes, were embarrassing her in public.

Samantha had an image to maintain among her peer group. She was one of the leaders in her eleventh-grade class. To have her parents speak to her like that in public was damaging to that image. If someone she knew overheard them there would be hell to pay when she returned to school. Even more importantly her standing in the group would suffer. Evelyn was second in command so to speak and would surely jump at the chance to humiliate her. In Samantha's opinion Evelyn was the green-eyed bitch in the group and something like this would give her license to bring Samantha down a peg or two.

Samantha's mother continued speaking.

"You do have a life. However, being sixteen doesn't make you a grown woman to make decisions that are contrary to the rules of the house."

At that moment the young boy who was seated across his father interrupted matters. In a childish voice he asked for more ice cream.

"No," his mother snapped in response.

"Look at the mess you made of yourself already. Do you really think you deserve anymore?" she added.

The boy looked down at the white tee shirt he was wearing. There was a sorrowful look on his face and tears began to roll down. The boy's mother got up and escorted him to the rear of the restaurant toward the restroom. She bore a look of disgust as she moved through the crowd.

After the family were reunited, they remained silent and barely looked at one another. Their waiter came over and asked if they wanted anything else. In her mind she couldn't wait for them to leave and only asked because she had to as part of the responsibilities of her job.

After paying the bill Wesley had to use the restroom and he asked Gayle to give him a few minutes.

Next to each of the three faucets were a stack of neatly folded white paper towels and individual bottles of antibacterial hand soap. The walls and bathroom floor resembled a high-priced hotel in its décor. Wesley crossed the floor and entered the last stall. He had a rule and would avoid urinals whenever possible. They never gave him the privacy that he wanted or expected. Back in the day he always felt that someone was curious about the next man's "equipment" even though they were staring straight ahead. Conversely the barriers that separated each stall gave him the comfort that he sought during a very personal moment. The stall was free from any messages that he had seen in the past. Some were funny while others were downright filthy.

Wesley was standing in front of the toilet as his mind began to drift. He was not focused on any particular topic; it was a matter of a thousand images running through his mind all at once. In his mind's eye Wesley visualized faces of people that he did not recognize. Their muffled voices filled his head but he couldn't make out what they were saying. Wesley tried his best to ignore what was happening however the feeling was dangerously overpowering.

After relieving himself Wesley went to the sink and began washing his hands. He looked in the mirror and saw a reflection staring back at him the he didn't recognize. Wesley rubbed his eyes with his left and right hands hoping that would return him to a place that he knew. He looked closer at the reflection and noticed a pair of bloodshot eyes staring back at him. There were small red veins running through the whites of the person's eyes.

His temples throbbed.

Wesley splashed a handful of cold water on his face which momentarily helped to relieve the pain he was feeling. However, a few seconds later his left eye began to tremble. He could feel his eyelids flutter as if controlled by some unknown force. Wesley had no idea how much time had passed.

Another splash of water and the physical anomaly passed as if it had never occurred. His sense of recognition thankfully returned.

"Now what the hell was that all about?" Wesley asked himself. He wondered if there was something seriously wrong with him. His breathing was slightly accelerated and he could feel his heart beating against his chest. Wesley turned around and leaned back against the sink in an effort to stabilize himself. There was no way in hell that he could face Gayle in this condition. He faced the mirror once more and looked at his reflection. There were small beads of sweat dotting his forehead which he wiped away.

As Wesley exited the restroom, he wrestled with the thought on whether he should say anything to Gayle about what had just happened. He heard stories about people having a stroke and dropping dead without any warning and as the Lord was his witness, that scared him more than anything. However, all things considered he was feeling much better and decided to keep things to himself for now. There was no sense in getting Gayle worked up especially since he wasn't sure exactly what had happened. He was no doctor Wesley joked to himself.

Dr. McCain said that everything was fine, didn't he? With that in mind Wesley decided to leave it alone for the time being. He wanted to get home as quickly as possible. There was a football game on that he wanted to watch.

The ride home was nothing like the one that Gayle suffered through on their way into the city. This time Wesley was a virtual chatter box. He couldn't stop taking about one subject or another. He went on and on as if he hadn't spoken a word in years. Gayle didn't mind because she enjoyed the physical as well as the verbal company.

Without realizing it Gayle took a hold of her husband's hand and lightly gave it a squeeze.

The smile on her face spoke volumes.

Two days had come and gone since their technological disaster had occurred. Thomas was the right man for the job. He was able to retrieve ninety-five percent of the lost data which was huge. The man literally pulled their asses out of the proverbial frying pan.

Victoria recalled Thomas' last words that she should contact him if there were any other issues or if she had any questions. Victoria was not the type to read something into nothing. Yet she couldn't help wonder if Thomas was in some roundabout way suggesting something more on a personal level. It was time to put her thoughts into action. Without any further procrastination Victoria punched in Thomas' extension.

He answered on the second ring.

Victoria introduced herself and began the conversation by thanking Thomas for the job he had done.

"Not a problem," Thomas responded.

"I appreciate the vote of confidence," he added.

Victoria decided that she would stay on point for a few moments and then move the conversation in a different direction.

"Actually, I was surprised that you were available. I know how busy it can get down in your area so . . ."

"To be honest. Between you and me I've been looking for a challenge from a technical standpoint and the systems in your department came right on time," Thomas said as if he would receive the good citizen's award if he were successful.

"Were things really that bad?" Victoria asked in a humorous manner.

"I didn't have to call in for backup so that's a good thing," Thomas said matching Victoria's humor.

"Well since you put it that way, I'm glad that we were able to accommodate you," Victoria responded.

Thomas didn't know anything about Victoria or her area in the company prior to her call for help. But for whatever reason, right now he felt a connection. There was no reason that he shouldn't ask her out as one professional to another. The idea persisted in spite of the fact that the last time he went on a date, things hadn't gone as planned. In fact, it was a disaster. Laughable now but a disaster just the same.

Thomas believed he said the right things when he met Tabatha. But honestly it boiled down to one hard cold fact. They simply never clicked. Although they parted on good terms it still left a sour taste in his mouth as well as a slight feeling of failure.

His date with Tabatha was more than a year ago and for what it was worth Thomas felt that enough time had passed and this may be his chance to get back into the game so to speak. Just don't appear desperate Thomas told himself. This time he was being serious.

"I might be taking a chance here," Thomas began. The telephone receiver felt slightly moist in his left hand.

"But would you like to go out for a drink sometime this week?" Thomas felt slightly awkward but he was not going to let past experiences stop him from following his emotions. From the little that he learned about Victoria she was light years away from Tabatha in every positive meaning of the word.

"I think that's a great idea," Victoria responded.

"As long as you let me buy the first round. It's the least I can do considering the fact that you made me look like a shining star."

"I'm pretty sure that's not the case, but I'll take the compliment just the same. How does Friday sound?" Thomas asked taking note that his self-confidence was on the rise.

"Do you know Sevens on Lexington Avenue?" Thomas asked.

"I think so," Victoria responded.

"How does six o'clock sound?" Thomas asked.

"Perfect. I'm looking forward to it," Victoria said. There was a tone of excitement in her response that Victoria hoped Thomas didn't pick up on.

They agreed on Friday.

After the conversation ended Victoria took a moment to bask in the glow of what had just happened. She found that speaking with Thomas came easier than she expected. There was something about the tone of his voice that seemed to invite an unsolicited conversation. She could imagine Thomas standing on any street corner and total strangers coming up to ask for directions. Maybe he had that kind of face or that special personality that people gravitated toward. Whatever it was, Victoria liked it.

In the very same breath Victoria thought she could be reaching for a version of the man that may not exist. Did anyone really find romance solely based on an initial feeling? It takes a lot more than that if it's going to work. Patience, sharing and understanding were chief among the mixture that made any meaningful relationship last.

Victoria thought of her parents and the ups and downs they must have endured but managed to keep their marriage afloat and thriving.

Victoria looked inward and realized there was no reward for living her life in an emotional bubble. Whether she chose to admit it or not there was something about Thomas that she wanted to explore.

Nothing ventured nothing gained Victoria thought.

Victoria spent the better part of the morning on the telephone, faxing documents and sending text messages. Thankfully there were no interruptions and the day ended with her accomplishing more than she imagined. As for her last official act of the day Victoria arranged several files on her desk, made one last call and then left the office.

As the elevator made its decent toward the lobby Victoria's thoughts turned to her plans for the evening. She didn't feel like cooking and decided to pick up some takeout. Victoria recalled spending time teaching Jasmine how to use the chopsticks that routinely came with their meal. The idea was to get the food into her mouth before it fell back onto her plate. Victoria patiently watched as Jasmine's frustration rose with each attempt. Ultimately Jasmine gave up and chose to complete her meal with the tools of the trade that she knew the best.

Victoria wanted to call her parents but fatigue took a stranglehold on her and sapped what little strength she had left. Making her way upstairs Victoria checked on Jasmine before proceeding down the hallway to her bedroom. Each night before settling in Victoria peeked into Jasmine's room to make sure everything was all right. Not that she ever believed anything bad was going to happen it was all about being able to sleep peacefully through the night. When she was younger Jasmine sometimes pretended to be asleep. Victoria was able to notice because she couldn't stop her eyes from moving. It was a game that they played every once in a while, and each got a tremendous kick out of it.

Now within the comfort of her bedroom Victoria had time to relax and think of brighter things to come.

Namely her …

Victoria paused in mid thought. She was not ready to think of her rendezvous with Thomas as date. But she was unsure if that was not the correct label.

She wondered what Thomas thought it was.

In the end Victoria decided that it didn't really matter what type of label either had prepared. From what she could sense during their conversation they were looking forward to enjoying each other's company and the rest would take care of itself.

The working hours that made up Thursday and Friday seemed to breeze by without much notice. Everything that Victoria was involved in went off without a hitch. It had to be karma working in her favor and perhaps she should take a chance and buy a lottery ticket Victoria humored herself.

Victoria inhaled and exhaled deeply as she stepped into an empty elevator car. As the doors closed, she must have checked her watch and makeup at least three times during the descent. As the elevator moved downward other occupants from the buildings lower floors began to board.

There were multiple conversations regarding plans for the weekend. Overall, getting out of the city and seeing family, friends or hanging out at a club dominated their itinerary. Victoria was feeling a little anxious about seeing Thomas as the car passed the fourth and then the third floors. She silently chastised herself for thinking like a school girl that was going out with the captain of the football team on her first date. She was much too old and mature to react that way. By the time the elevator doors opened Victoria had it all together—or so she hoped.

Victoria spotted Thomas from across the lobby floor. He was in one of the shops that sold everything from newspapers to books to New York labeled gifts. He was browsing through the political science section. An odd choice of reading material Victoria thought for someone that appeared to be wrapped up in the world of technology.

Victoria was not exactly sure what to say when she approached him. Humor was usually a good ice breaker when it came to charting unknown waters. Although Victoria never considered herself as a comedian of any kind, but her less than formidable attempt worked with Raymond when they first met.

"Here I am. Ready to get this show on the road?" Victoria asked in a humorous manner.

"I'm looking forward to the evening and I'm as ready as I'm ever going to be," Thomas responded extending his right hand in greeting.

The handshake lasted a few seconds longer than each recipient had intended.

"When I made our reservations, I found out that tonight there's going to be a live jazz band during dinner. Is that alright with you?" he asked.

Thomas studied Victoria's expression to gauge her reaction to the revelation that their outing would include a sit-down meal. Something he had neglected to mention when he initially asked her out.

When he took a second to recall their conversation Victoria did mention something about buying the first round. But was he being presumptuous in thinking that dinner was a given?

Thomas wondered if his engine to make a positive impression stalled before it got out of the station.

In her mind Victoria didn't want to play the comparison game but Raymond was heavily into jazz also. While it wasn't necessarily her cup of tea in the beginning, over time, she began to appreciate it more and more.

"That sounds fine with me," Victoria responded.

"A close friend of mine was into jazz," she added with a smile on her face.

"Just remember the first round is on me and we can split the check for the meal. Deal?" she asked.

As Thomas and Victoria maneuvered their way through crowded pedestrian sidewalks, he made certain that she was on the inside from the curb. Thomas explained his reason. He said his father believed that when walking with a woman she should never be on the side close to the street. He said the same rule applied walking with a child.

"It bothered my father when parents walked several feet in front of their child expecting them to keep up. Little feet can't walk to the same beat he would say. I guess he was preaching safety on one hand and protection in the other. I imagine that in either situation it amounted to the same thing," Thomas said.

"Your father sounds like a special kind of man," Victoria remarked.

"He was. But don't get me wrong like anyone else he had a different side also," Thomas said in a matter-of-fact tone.

A flash of her father's disposition over the years came to Victoria's mind.

"Well, here we are," Thomas said as he held the door open for

Victoria. There was a decent crowd inside even for what many New Yorkers would consider as having an early evening.

The host asked if they wanted a seat at the bar, a booth or a table. After requesting a table Thomas and Victoria were led to the other side of the floor. Victoria was seated first. The lighting in the dining area was soft yet bright enough to see and appreciate the artwork and photographs that hung on the walls. There were political, film and sports personalities all photographed while showing off their best smile. Exquisite marble sculptures of Greek gods rested on pedestals in each corner of the floor. Their features were smooth and captured the emotion on their face as well as their muscular bodily features.

"I take it you've been here on more than one occasion?" Victoria asked as she adjusted the napkin in her lap.

"Once before about a year ago at the recommendation by a friend from grad school. I came in for a drink just to check the place out and wound up staying for the performance. I have to say that my journey into jazz started years ago when I went to my first concert," Thomas confessed.

"Sadly, my vices lean closer to Fifth and Madison Avenues where most of my shopping takes place," Victoria said as if revealing a once hidden fault.

"How often is that?" Thomas asked as he examined the sheepish look on Victoria's face.

"It depends on the occasion and the level of stress that I had to deal with during the day. I can't recall her name but some famous woman once said that pampering yourself was a cure for whatever ails you," Victoria said with a smile.

"Well judging by the outfit that you have on it seems that you treat yourself very well," Thomas commented.

"Why Thomas," Victoria began. "Flattery like that will get you everywhere."

When the waitress appeared to take their drink orders Victoria chose a Chablis and Thomas requested a single malt scotch. In his opinion single malt scotches were the cream of the crop and any other spirit played a distant second.

Thomas lifted his glass in Veronica's direction.

"Here's to the things in life that only make you stronger and wiser."

"I could not have said it any better," Victoria responded with her glass raised in kind.

After several minutes of small talk had passed the waitress reappeared and asked if they were ready to order their entree or if they needed additional time.

Coincidently they both decided on the grilled salmon. Secretly each took that as a good sign.

"I noticed you didn't request any vegetables with your meal," Victoria commented.

"Pretty sharp of you. To be honest vegetables and I don't get along much. We've had this love and hate relationship for as long as I can remember," Thomas confessed.

A look of doubt appeared on Victoria's face.

"Would you believe I held my breath until my mother gave up on trying to make me eat anything green?" Thomas offered.

"It couldn't have been that bad," Victoria said with the same expression of doubt on her face.

"On the contrary. You've never met my mother," Thomas responded.

Victoria recalled her youth when it came to the family sitting down at the dinner table and her dislike for something on her plate.

"You have yet to meet mine," Victoria countered as her left eyebrow rose in an expression of emphasis.

When their meals arrived each plate was covered with a two-inch metal shield that served to seal in the flavor and temperature. Victoria imagined that this was one of those extra touches that Thomas had mentioned earlier. Again, Victoria was impressed with the level of service that the restaurant provided. This might be a great place to bring Sharon and the gang the next time they decide to go out after work. The weird part of it all was the chance of running into Thomas on one of those nights. Victoria would have more explaining to do than she wanted, with the exception of Sharon of course. It was all a roll of the dice that Victoria was willing to take and for better or for worse live with the results.

Thomas and Victoria spent time after dinner reminiscing about their past life experiences, which mercifully didn't include work.

"I relocated from the west coast ten years ago with two-hundred dollars in my pocket. I kicked around from one job to the next wondering where I was going to wind up," Thomas began.

"Initially I swore that I would never leave San Francisco and my beloved football team. But somewhere along the line I realized that I needed a change, not only of scenery but my lifestyle. A complete makeover if you will. So I headed east," Thomas said.

"I put some feelers out and landed a position with a consulting firm based in Baltimore before deciding to test my chops and try New York on for size. So much had changed and I decided that there were things I needed to experience if I wanted the success in life that I sought," Thomas offered.

"I'm not sure I follow," Victoria said.

"It's a little hard to explain but I decided early on that I wanted to make it on my own without being a financial or emotional burden on my parents. I'm sure they felt otherwise but the feeling of self-accomplishment really ate at me and the time came when I had to do something about it."

Thomas wondered if he had given away too much of himself especially on their first outing away from work. However, Victoria didn't appear to be bored at his ramblings and on the positive side he was being honest. Thomas didn't want anything that he said to come back and bite him on the ass. Lies in life always have a way of catching up with an individual with devastating results when they came to light.

"What about the other members of your family?" Victoria asked. "Any sisters or brothers?"

"I had an older sister but she passed away when we were kids," Thomas said as he looked into Victoria's eyes.

"I'm so sorry to hear that," Victoria said. "Was she sick?"

"Sick? No, it was nothing like that, but that's a story for another time," Thomas answered.

Thomas took a sip from his drink followed by some of the glass of iced water in front of him. Actually, he was stalling for time to see if Victoria would volunteer any information about her past, present or future.

One thousand one. One thousand two. One thousand three, he mentally counted.

"How about you?" Thomas asked. "What tales of wonder might you have to share?"

"Tales yes," Victoria said enthusiastically. "Wonders not so much," she added in a humorous manner that was accompanied by a bright smile.

"When I'm not at work most of my time is spent with my daughter Jasmine," Victoria said.

After revealing the fact that she had a child Victoria studied Thomas' expression. Victoria understood that she was being silly but she knew of situations where children changed everything and *"Mr. Perfect"* bailed the first chance he got.

To put her thought process to the test, Victoria opened up about her history. However, she left out the part about her dad's health issues. As Thomas alluded to earlier, some things were better left for another time. Thomas asked about Jasmine and if she were anything like her mother. It appeared that Thomas was genuinely interested in hearing all about their mother and daughter relationship.

"In some respects yes, Jasmine is exactly like me. But then in others she has a personality all of her own. They say that children take the best of their parents and then put their own spin on things. Jasmine has a wide range of interests. But as far as her following in my footsteps, that's so far down the road I haven't given it much thought. Jasmine's a great kid but at the same time she can be quite a handful," Victoria said.

"I don't have any firsthand experience, but I've heard children can be a blessing under the right circumstances. It's something that I firmly believe," Thomas responded.

There was a clear tone of sincerity in his voice that was not lost on Victoria. If there were a relationship to be had at some point in the future then Thomas was definitely checking off all the right boxes.

After finishing their dinner Thomas and Victoria each toyed with the idea of having dessert. The chocolate covered cheesecake the waitress mentioned earlier was tempting as they both admitted to having a sweet tooth. Victoria decided to stick to her guns and forgo dessert. Thomas on the other hand couldn't resist anything related to chocolate. The look on his face told the story when the waitress reappeared with his plate. The added dollop of whipped cream and sliced strawberry was a nice touch.

The pair spent the next two hours getting to know one another a little better while enjoying the sounds of tonight's entertainment *Transitions Peak.* The band featured a saxophone player who worked his instrument as if he had taken lessons from the time he could walk.

The band entertained the crowd with an assortment of classics from the 70's, the 80's while working their way up to the sounds of today. There were solos by each band member that got better and better to the crowd's delight. They attacked their respective instruments with unbridled joy as they had done so many times in the past. Each artist whipped the crowd into a frenzy in an apparent attempt to outdo the player before him. It was all in fun and each player paid respect to the other when their solo performance had ended. The last solo was by the flutist. He moved and danced around the stage as if he were floating on air. With the final rendering of his solo, he brought the band back together with a crashing crescendo that could have brought the dead back to life. Thomas confessed that he never saw anything like this in spite of the number of jazz concerts he'd attended over the years. He was glad to see that Victoria was enjoying herself as she moved her body to the hypnotic beat and drummed her fingers on the table.

When the band ended their set there was not an occupied seat in the audience. The standing ovation was deafening and seemed to go on forever. There were boisterous calls for more from the crowd which were just as loud as their initial applause.

Transitions Peak responded by rewarding their new found fan base with a tune from their latest CD titled *"Uncharted Bliss."*

"Now that's what I call entertainment," Thomas said. "Kind of makes you want to immediately add them to your playlist and buy anything they have recorded."

"I have to admit at first I was a little skeptical, but any doubts were quickly erased," Victoria confessed.

Thomas lifted his half empty glass in Victoria's direction in agreement.

There was a momentary lull in the conversation so Thomas took advantage of the opportunity and returned to something Victoria had mentioned earlier in the evening.

"I was just thinking about your daughter and wondered who has the babysitting chores tonight?" Thomas asked.

"My parents of course," Victoria responded. "I don't think I could trust her with anyone else," Victoria said.

At the mention of her daughter, Victoria fought off the urge to look at her watch believing it would send a signal to Thomas that she was ready to end the evening. However, that was not the case at all. The honest truth was that she could have spent so much more time talking with Thomas no matter what the subject involved.

"Perhaps you should give your parents a call just to check in," Thomas suggested.

"Would you mind?" Victoria asked. She was again taken off guard by Thomas' level of concern.

"Not at all. Family always comes first," he said.

After Victoria ended her call, she told Thomas that everything was fine and Jasmine was on her best behavior.

"Are you up for a second round?" Thomas asked.

"Well considering that I turned down dessert, I don't mind if I do," Victoria responded.

Thomas noticed that their waiter was standing a few feet away. He got her attention and tilted his empty glass in the air along with two fingers. The waitress smiled back in Thomas' direction acknowledging his request.

"You know all the tricks of the trade," Victoria said. "What other feats of magic do you have up your sleeve?" she asked.

"I gave up pulling rabbits out of top hats a long time ago because that seemed too passé considering what modern-day illusionists are doing today. Right now I'm working on reading minds," Thomas offered with a smile.

"And how is that going for you?" Victoria inquired eagerly wondering what kind of response Thomas was going to pull out of the air as it were.

Thomas shook the blade of his right hand from side to side as if to say so-so.

"Care for a demonstration?" he asked in a confident tone.

"Are you going to try and read my mind right now?" Victoria asked obviously not putting much stock in Thomas' mind reading abilities.

"Now that wouldn't be fair. You appear to be much too complicated a read, especially on a first date," Thomas said.

"Oh, is that what this is a first date?" Victoria asked recalling how the same question plagued her thoughts earlier in the day.

"Let's not put a label on it just yet. Perhaps I used the wrong word," Thomas quickly responded.

Victoria decided that she wasn't going to let Thomas off the hook just yet.

"Mind reading huh?" she said. "If you're not willing to try it out on me, then how about someone in the crowd," Victoria urged.

"Are you serious?" Thomas asked. "I'm a little rusty and I've been out of practice for some time now."

"I'm not expecting miracles mind you, a simple demonstration will do just fine," Victoria said in a challenging tone.

"Okay here we go," Thomas began. "Keep your eye on the couple two tables away." With the index and middle fingers of his left and right hand moving in a slow circular pattern on his temples. Seconds later Thomas seemed to go into a self-induced trance.

Victoria watched in disbelief at Thomas' antics thinking the man must be out of his mind or he was working too hard for a laugh. Victoria was enjoying the performance and decided she would play along with whatever prediction Thomas offered.

Thomas decided that if she wanted a show then he would give Victoria her full money's worth. Behind his closed eyes Thomas began to quietly hum a tune before speaking.

"Today is the young lady's birthday—her twenty-eighth or close to it. They're going to bring out a chocolate cake. With a single burning candle," he said.

Thomas paused momentarily for effect.

"Her name is Mary," he added before becoming silent.

"Ok," Victoria began. "You can stop any time now. I haven't had that many drinks," she playfully added.

"You doubt the abilities of Thomas the Great? Shame on you. While I haven't solved any great mysteries yet, I've been known to find a lost pet or two from time to time," Thomas empathically said in his defense.

As part of the routine Victoria followed Thomas' instructions that she keep her eyes on the couple he had mentioned.

Moments later and much to Victoria's amazement a crew of waiters brought over a chocolate covered cake with a single burning candle to the couple's table. They burst into a shaky rendition of the happy birthday song. They also mentioned her name in the song.

Victoria's head slumped downward.

"All right. I'm impressed," Victoria said again eagerly waiting to see what Thomas was going to say.

"How in the world did you manage that?" she asked.

There was a wide smile on Thomas' face that he was not able to contain even if he were offered a king's ransom.

"I'll tell you this much," Thomas began. Both arms were held up chest high with palms facing outward. His head was slightly turned to one side.

"Neither one is a friend of mine and I haven't seen them before tonight," Thomas swore.

By that time the waitress had arrived with their drinks. She removed the empty glasses and placed the fresh drinks in front of them.

"Will there be anything else?" she asked.

"No thank you," Thomas responded.

"Okay. I have to admit that was pretty darn impressive," Victoria began. "Now that the trick is over you can tell me the secret." Victoria pressed.

"You mean you're not going to ask me to try it again? Thomas innocently asked. "Most people do you know," he added obviously feeling good about himself.

"I would if I still didn't think the whole thing was some kind of prearranged setup," Victoria said with a heightened sense of suspicion.

"Not much into the paranormal are you?" Thomas asked.

The question involuntarily brought a smile to Victoria's face and a barely audible laugh escaped from within.

"I had a crazy yet interesting experience in college," Victoria began. "After that I put my Ouija Board away for good."

"Anything else you'd like to share?" Thomas asked as he shifted his seated position. "Your secrets are safe with me," he added with his right hand extended upward as if taking an oath of office.

"Easy there big fellah," Victoria warned. "A girl can't divulge all of her secrets at once. There has to be some element of surprise and mystery you know. But if you want to tell me about that little birthday thing, I'm all ears," she added.

Once again, a smile creased Thomas' face before he began speaking.

"It's all about being observant," Thomas confessed. "If I really had any mind reading abilities I'd probably move to Vegas or Atlantic City to expand my meager bank account."

"Okay. But how does being an observant soul give you the inside track on what was happening two tables away?" Victoria inquired.

"Just before we were seated, I noticed a small shopping bag with a pink bow attached on the floor next to the guy's chair. I also noticed the confident look of a well-planned evening written all over his face. The rest was pure deduction and I determined that tonight had to be a special occasion."

"And from those little tidbits you came up with a birthday celebration?" Victoria quizzically asked.

"Based on the couple's age an anniversary didn't seem to fit. So ruling that out I realized that my choices were limited," Thomas said.

"Her name," Victoria said. "How in the world did you guess that her name was Mary?"

"That wasn't easy. But I noticed the diamond studded pin on her left lapel. I ruled out Margaret, Mia, Martha or any of the other names that began with the letter M and went for the most obvious one, Mary. But I have to admit that was purely guess work on my part. Sometimes I win but there are times where I'm not even in the ball park," Thomas confessed.

"Well with that ability of yours, I'm going to have to watch my p's and q's. You may have me totally figured out in a matter of days," Victoria said.

"Oh contraire," Thomas said. "Like I said earlier you're too much of a complicated read…but I like that."

"You got that right buster," Victoria said with a smile on her face while raising her glass in Thomas' direction.

Thomas and Victoria spent time talking about books, movies, religion and finally the political arena. They each had different and some similar views on each subject. But there was also a meeting of the mind on things that they wouldn't necessarily have agreed upon before getting to know one another. Perhaps if they each were with someone different, their mutual agreement may not have evolved.

As the evening continued to move on Victoria secretly admitted that she liked the way Thomas thought. She especially liked the fact that he didn't try to pawn off his ideas on her. Thomas let her have the floor so to speak when expressing her feelings and ideas. He was interesting, confident and logical in his thought process. In her circle of female friends so many complained that the majority of men they've known or dated were not as open minded. Of course, that kind of attack sometimes backfired leaving both parties with a feeling of bitterness and contempt for the other.

"What are your plans for the weekend?" Thomas asked. The plain and simple truth of the matter was that he wanted to spend as much time with Victoria before they went back to work and their separate lives. For all he knew tonight could have been a fluke and he may never experience this kind of bliss again for some time. Thomas had to consider the fact that although Victoria seemed to be enjoying herself and his company, she had a life of her own. She seemed extremely dedicated to her family and may not have the time or the urge to add dating into the mix. Of course, Thomas hoped this wasn't the case.

"Not that much," Victoria responded. "I forwarded some files to my personal email with the intention of looking them over, but I've been down that road before and never quite accomplished much of anything. Shameful isn't it?" Victoria said wryly.

"Not really," Thomas offered. "It all depends on how you look at it. From my point of view personal time and office time should never occupy the same space for any significant period of time. I look at both places as church and state. Never let the two interfere with a good time or one's level of sanity."

"Words to live by sir," Victoria said in a complimentary manner.

Victoria looked down at her watch and noticed that it was almost ten o'clock. She announced that it was best that they call it a night because she still had to pick up Jasmine from her parent's house.

"I figured as much," Thomas responded.

"Then I guess I'll see you on Monday?" Thomas said in a half question and half a statement kind of way.

"I hope so," Victoria responded. "I still have to get through the next two days," Victoria said with a smile.

As Thomas and Victoria exited the restaurant the night life of the city was in full swing. They were greeted with the sounds of traffic, blaring horns and flashing lights. The pair made their way back to their office building where the evening all started. Thomas escorted Victoria to the parking garage where a great evening would sadly come to an end.

Thomas said that he hoped they could do this again.

"I can't remember the last time had I had a better evening from beginning to end," Victoria offered. "And for sure we will do this again."

Victoria and Thomas parted ways after a handshake and an embrace. Thomas was parked two blocks away. He felt good about an evening which checked off all of the right points of his possibly building a relationship with Victoria. As far as he was concerned all signs appeared to say that good fortune was on his side. This was the first time in a very long time that Thomas wished the weekend ended before it actually began. Victoria had so much to do with his thought process in that regard.

Gayle had trouble falling to sleep. There were too many thoughts running through her head. However, when she did manage to sleep the joy and comfort only came in small increments. Wesley on the other hand had not suffered the same fate. Gayle rolled over onto her right side and looked at the small clock radio on the night table. She groaned at its digital face which read five-thirty. The fact that she had gone to bed at ten o'clock the night before meant very little. Usually with that much sleep under her belt Gayle was ready to tackle anything the morning had in store for her.

Trying not to disturb Wesley, Gayle sat up slowly and placed her feet on the carpeted floor. She guided them into her slippers and crept out of the bedroom not bothering to take a second look at her husband. As Gayle made her way down each step of the staircase, she said a silent prayer thanking the Lord for allowing her to witness the coming of another day.

As she entered the kitchen Gayle decided that it was much too early for breakfast and settled for a cup of coffee. Black. This was not the way she usually had her coffee but considering the night she had perhaps a strong cup of coffee would help her make it through the next few hours, or at least until she was her old self.

Moments after Gayle sat down and breathed in the intoxicating aroma of her morning beverage, a loud scream of pain rained down from the floor above. The cry seemed to radiate throughout the entire house. It was as if someone were being mercilessly tortured. Gayle jumped to her feet knocking over the cup and saucer in one motion. Both hit the tiled floor and the resulting sound appeared to be magnified a thousand-fold.

Gayle raced upstairs taking the steps two at a time. She honestly had no idea that she could move so fast. But under the circumstances her body reacted without much thought of what she had accomplished.

"Wesley," Gayle called out as she entered the bedroom. She was slightly out of breath. There was no immediate sight of her husband. Gayle called out his name once again only to be met by silence. The palms of her hands were cold and wet as if they had been immersed in water.

Her heart slammed uncontrollably behind her breast. However, in a flash of clarity Gayle noticed a light leaking from beneath the bathroom door.

"Wesley," Gayle called out again. This time there was an unmistakable trembling in her voice and she realized that it would take a moment to regain her composure.

"Wesley are you in there?" Gayle asked softly.

Gayle was standing outside of the bathroom door with her ear pressed against its painted wooden frame. She knocked lightly hoping for a response.

"Who the hell is that?" responded a voice from the other side. It was nothing like the voice of the man she had spent the last thirty-five years married to. Its tone was cold and menacing.

"Wesley open the door," Gayle said as she turned the doorknob frantically from left to right hoping it was unlocked.

No such luck.

"Get away from here and leave me alone. I don't know you," Wesley shouted back to what he deemed to be a stranger.

Gayle could hear the confusion in her husband's voice and she could only imagine the complicated thoughts that were running rampant within the halls of his mind.

Gayle listened closely. She could hear a deep throated humming radiating from inside the bathroom. The tune was rambling and without rhythm or reason. The pitch changed several times from high to low and back again.

Suddenly there was a crashing sound of broken glass followed by another howl of pain.

"Wesley for God's sake open the door right now," Gayle shouted. It was a conscious effort of Gayle's never to take the name of the Lord in vain no matter what the circumstances were. However, at the moment the words jumped out of her mouth before she could pull them back.

From her side of the door Gayle could hear Wesley pacing back and forth. Gayle wondered what on earth Wesley could have broken. The only glass objects in the bathroom were the mirrored doors of the medicine cabinet and the window. She wondered if Wesley were attempting some sort of escape by crawling through the small window above the bathtub.

For the next several moments there was no sound coming from the other side of the door. All movement had stopped as well as the humming. The silence worried Gayle more than the rambling sounds her husband had made earlier.

"Wesley come on out of there. We need to talk." Gayle's tone was calming and inviting in its delivery. Her goal was to try and coax her husband to leave the bathroom.

"I'm about to start breakfast," Gayle said knowing this was Wesley's favorite meal of the day. But at the same time, she felt silly recommending a meal considering the situation. But her words were born from the fact that she didn't know what else to say at the moment.

Wesley called back to his wife.

"You're trying to poison me," Wesley responded. "You tried it before and I know you're going to try it again if you get the chance. I'm smarter than that you know," Wesley yelled back.

Again, Gayle took note that the voice coming back was nothing like her husband's. The anger and confusion were still present.

"Wesley please come out of there right now," Gayle pleaded with a heightened sense of urgency. However, her pleas only seemed to agitate Wesley even more.

"Leave me the hell alone. I don't want anything to do with you!"

This time Wesley's response was accompanied by fists pounding against the door as the anger in his voice increased in its intensity.

Gayle was frightened for his safety not knowing what Wesley might do to himself. She also had to consider what he was capable of doing if she pressed him too far. Would he really physically attack her and if he did how would she protect herself?

"I want to go home," Wesley said emphatically. "I don't belong here. "If you think you can keep me locked up and away from my family you had better guess again!"

Seconds later Gayle heard the sound of the shower curtain crashing downward as if it were pulled from its perch. Gayle wondered if Wesley was indeed trying to escape through the window. Gayle realized that in his state of mind she wouldn't put it past him. Her thoughts turned to the evergreen bushes that they had put in last year. The idea was to dress up the front of the house as a measure of curb appeal and security. If Wesley had tried to escape that way, at the very least he would suffer a few cuts and bruises. This was something Gayle knew she could deal with as long as it brought Wesley back to his right state of mind.

"You are home," Gayle responded. "Look around you. Don't you see anything familiar? Every morning you stand in front of that mirror shaving your face. You've been brushing your teeth with the same toothbrush for more months than I can remember. I bought you two new ones. Red and white."

Gayle stopped for a moment hoping that her words would ring a tone of familiarity and Wesley would snap back into reality.

"Look at the rack against the wall. Don't you see two towels with our initials engraved on them? They were Christmas presents from your granddaughter Jasmine. Think about the watch that you have on your wrist. A watch that you swore never to take off even when you slept. It was a birthday present from your daughter Victoria."

Gayle made it a point to use names that Wesley would hopefully recognize and perhaps that would help bring him back.

"Who?" Wesley angrily responded. "I know you're trying to confuse me with your words and that's not going to work either. Not now, not ever."

It frightened Gayle even more that Wesley's mind appeared to abandon everything that he had previously and unconditionally cherished. Not even the mention of his daughter or his grandchild seemed to lift the dark mental cloud that he was under. Gayle began to realize she was running out of options and would have to call someone.

The police? Dr. McCain? Victoria?

"You better get away from me or I'm liable to hurt you," Wesley said. Again, he pounded his fists against the back of the door. Gayle could see the hinges jump in response to his physical attack. At this point Gayle was beyond mere concern and she was actually afraid of her husband. The fact that he was not responsible would not weaken the physical harm that he might inflict on her.

Gayle chose to call Victoria. Dealing with Wesley in this state was not something she could handle on her own. There was very little doubt that she needed as much help as possible.

But suppose Victoria wasn't available? Suppose she was out with Jasmine somewhere or the other? Calling the police on her husband was another option, but every fiber of her being said that it was not the right one. It was obvious that her pleas to Wesley were doing more harm than good. Gayle couldn't stand the thought that if she did nothing and Wesley had hurt himself, her sense of guilt would be overwhelming.

"Wesley I'm going to call Victoria. I really don't want to bother her but you're not leaving me with much of a choice."

Wesley didn't immediately respond. But then.

"Who's out there with you?" Wesley asked. His voice was far less threatening. At least that was something to look forward to Gayle thought. Could it be that he was coming back to his senses or was he playing a game that was the by-product of a twisted and disturbed mind? Gayle envisioned her husband standing or sitting on the edge of the tub or the closed toilet seat with a mind working and planning his next move.

Gayle wondered if she could face Wesley, even if his mind had cleared. What would stop him from verbally abusing her once again? Gayle realized that she had no answer to the questions considering her present reality.

Last month Wesley had unintentionally soiled himself. Gayle remembered that they were both standing in the living room talking about rearranging the furniture. In the middle of his sentence a stream of liquid began running down his leg. The odd part of it was that he didn't seem to notice what had happened until she brought it to his attention. After realizing what he had done Gayle noticed the look of embarrassment etched on his face. Wesley bolted out of the room without saying another word. After Wesley had cleaned himself up there was never any mention of the incident again.

Gayle knew that during their life some guys woke up fully erect. But as far as she was concerned, Wesley was well past the age of not being in control of his bodily functions. Horny teen-aged boys yes but not a full-grown man.

At the time Gayle was faced with an entirely different set of issues. In the past Wesley's shortcomings were for the most part victimless but now there was so much more at stake.

"Wesley are you ready to come out now?" Gayle pleaded. She held the cordless phone in her hand knowing that at any moment she would have to call Victoria and enlist her help. Worrying that she may be interrupting her daughter so early on a Saturday morning no longer mattered.

This was about family and Gayle was sure that Victoria would completely understand without any reservations.

Gayle knocked on the door. The only thing she could hear in response was sound of water from the faucet at the sink.

On.

Off. On.

Off…

It was as if someone had just discovered its use and was fascinated with the operation.

When the humming returned, Gayle was left to wonder if Wesley was about to drift further away into a senseless void. If that were the case then they would be back to square one. Gayle couldn't wait much longer and without any further delay she began to punch in Victoria's cell number. She was partially facing the bedroom window. Just as Gayle was about the press the final three digits on the keypad, her movement stopped when she noticed a stream of light escape from the bathroom. The door appeared to further open in slow motion. Gayle watched as Wesley's head peek out as if he were afraid of being caught doing something wrong. Gayle was momentarily trapped in limbo. Her first instinct was to run over to her husband and embrace him like she had never done before. Another part of her wanted to slap him across the face for what he had just put her through. As far as she cared either decision would have been appropriate. She also believed that no one in their right mind would blame her if she chose the latter. Gayle turned around and faced the bedroom window.

"Gayle what are you doing standing there looking out the window? The sun is barely up," Wesley said in a matter-of-fact tone.

Before turning around Gayle discretely slipped the cordless phone into the right pocket of her bathrobe.

"What am I doing?" Gayle asked. "Do you have any idea what I've been going through for the past twenty minutes?" There was a fair measure of anger in Gayle's voice. However, she quickly realized she had better put herself in check before Wesley's mental imbalance returned. Although for the life of her Gayle couldn't imagine things getting much worse than they were now.

In response to Gayle's question a look of confusion appeared on

Wesley's face as he stepped from behind the bathroom door. It was clear that he had no idea what his wife was talking about.

"The last thing I remember was getting out of bed and relieving myself," Wesley answered.

This was not the response Gayle had expected. Not that she expected Wesley to remember what had occurred, but she wanted more than the weak response he just delivered.

"Wesley look at yourself," Gayle said almost as if she were chastising a child. "Look down at your feet," she added without much of a change in the tone of her voice.

Wesley wondered what Gayle was talking about. There was nothing wrong with him. But he had learned from past experiences that he should go along with whatever game Gayle was playing. At least to keep the peace.

When Wesley looked down at his feet, he could see a trail of blood leading from the bathroom. He raised his right and left leg one after the other and inspected the bottom of each one. It was then that he noticed the source of the stain. His expression quickly changed from confusion to shock and back again. His bottom lip quivered uncontrollably.

"Don't you feel that?" Gayle asked while gesturing downward toward Wesley's feet.

Wesley tried to force his brain to process what his eyes were seeing.

"What happened, did I break something?" Wesley asked in a tone which said he no idea what had occurred during the twenty minutes Gayle just mentioned.

Blood on the floor and covering the bottom of his feet, what was going on here?

Wesley turned around and stepped back into the bathroom. He focused on the shattered mirror above the sink. Then turning his head slightly to the right Wesley noticed the shower curtain laying in the tub. The window was wide open. Wesley was frightened but he didn't want to show it. He was after all a grown man who was not supposed to show emotion no matter what the circumstances involved. However, raging inside his frame was a ball of confusion waiting to burst free.

"Gayle," he called out from the bathroom. "What happened in here?" he asked while pointing to the bathroom floor.

Gayle had to remain calm for both of them in spite of every fiber of her being wanting to yell and scream. But that was no solution and would only compound the shock that she saw in Wesley's eyes.

"That's not important right now. Come over here for a moment," Gayle said as she slowly guided Wesley to the bed and gently eased him down onto the mattress.

"Lets' get you cleaned up first then we can deal with what happened later," she said.

Wesley's thoughts were still slightly out of focus, but he didn't attempt to fight Gayle's suggestion.

As Gayle pulled off each of his socks, she could see that small pieces of glass were embedded in the sole of Wesley's feet.

"Don't move," Gayle ordered. "I need to get some antiseptic before this gets infected."

"But . . ." Wesley began. However, before he could get started again, Gayle cut him off with the wave of her hand. She moved to bathroom. With the bottom of her foot Gayle brushed away the shards of glass on the floor and reached down in the lower cabinet for the bottle of alcohol, tweezers, cotton balls and several gauze pads.

Momentarily alone with her thoughts Gayle tried her best not to break down in tears. Although it appeared that her husband was indeed losing his mind right in front of her, Gayle had to remain strong. But in the next few seconds Gayle could not hold back any longer. She felt the sensation of a warm liquid roll down her cheeks. It took a fair amount of will power for her not to look up into what was left of the mirror and see her reflection. It probably wouldn't help her focus on the task at hand.

"Gayle," Wesley called out. "Are you all right in there?"

Funny how things can change in a moment's notice Gayle thought. Not too long ago she was asking Wesley the very same question.

Through trembling lips Gayle responded. "I'm fine. I'll be there in just a minute. Just sit still," she added.

After Gayle had Wesley cleaned and bandaged, she didn't feel like doing much of anything else. Her mind had virtually shut down on itself. Wesley wouldn't stop asking questions about the scene in the bathroom and the root of the destruction inside. Gayle had no answers for him. At least not right now.

Gayle was in the process of finishing up in the bathroom. She worked in silence only responding to Wesley with a shrug here and there. She realized that the idea of one's mind betraying them had to be frightening when the world of reality eventually returned. But how on earth was she going to explain to her husband what had happened? How was she going to tell Wesley that he cursed her as if she were a stranger and during this episode, he had no memory of the other members in the family?

Gayle had no idea when the right time would be to tell someone they were no longer in control of their senses. News of that nature in her opinion boarded on the term "*Cruel and unusual punishment*."

Gayle returned to Wesley. She sat close to him on the bed.

"Is there something wrong with me?" Wesley asked as he turned to face his wife. As he posed the question Wesley noticed the look of hurt and pain in Gayle's face. Although he had no memory of what had happened, he felt that it must have been something unforgiveable. What in the world could he have put his wife through? She was the love of his life and so much more.

"Gayle," Wesley began. "Did I physically hurt you?" His voice was barely above a whisper and he could feel his lower lip tremble. Wesley knew that physically harming Gayle was well beyond his abilities. There were times when they were angry and had given each other the silent treatment, but that was pretty much the extent of their disagreements.

"I don't want to talk about it now," Gayle responded. She could only look in Wesley's direction for a few seconds at a time. The sense of hurt, anger and confusion were still fresh and traveling through her emotions with the speed of a runaway train.

"Gayle, we have to talk. If something happened then I have every right to know what it was, especially since I can see how it's bothering you." Wesley remained silent for a moment allowing his words to sink in. He was pretty sure if he kept at Gayle with his questions she would eventually open up.

But to her credit Gayle did not give in. She was unsure which emotion would take the lead if she answered without being careful.

Wesley took both of Gayle's hands into his. Hands that he knew too be soft yet strong. But at the moment they were hands that involuntarily trembled.

"Gayle, I love you," he began. "I'm not sure what happened but I want you to know that if I've said or done anything to cause you any pain, I'm sorry. We've been through ups and downs during our journey together and always managed to survive for the better. Agreed?"

A slight but noticeable smile of perhaps forgiveness appeared on Gayle's face. Although she did not break her silence, Wesley could see that his words may have had the desired effect he sought. Perhaps he was able to break down the emotionally constructed wall Gayle had built around herself. At least he had that much to be proud of when he measured the small victory against whatever may have happened.

Gayle didn't know what to make of the situation. Wesley's use of the word love felt warm and intoxicating. It had been years since she heard him speak that way and with such sincerity. Three simple words she thought. How powerful and how precious.

"I've got an idea," Wesley began as if it had been just another morning. "Why don't we go out for breakfast?"

Gayle simply smiled in agreement. For the time being they were once again a loving couple.

The day had gone so well that Victoria decided to leave a few hours early. She toyed with the idea of picking Jasmine up from school, but dismissed the thought deciding it would be better that she stick with her usual routine. The school bus driver would drop Jasmine at her parent's house and she would pick her up from there.

An hour later Victoria found herself browsing through the jazz section of Kingsbrooks Towers.

Kingsbrooks was a chain of stores that sold everything from music to appliances to electronics. She picked up the latest CD from the band that she and Thomas had enjoyed last week. It was a simple task but it played on her mind as if she were about to engage in an illegal act. It was out of the ordinary to say the least. The last time she purchased a gift for a man other than her father was for her late husband.

Victoria recalled the watch she purchased for his last birthday. It was a Swiss handcrafted piece made with yellow and white gold. Victoria recalled how much of a fuss Raymond made about the gift, swearing that he would wear it every day and give up the one he usually wore. The former treasure being an impressive Mentorim piece made in Italy. It could use a new band but was otherwise in excellent shape. Victoria thought about giving the watch to her father, but decided it would be better to keep it.

At times and alone with her thoughts Victoria wondered if Raymond were looking down on her. She wondered what he would think about her beginning a relationship with Thomas. Almost everyone she knew impressed upon her the need to move on and start dating. Victoria realized that it was an important part of getting her life back on track after such a devastating loss. But during those years Victoria convinced herself that she needed more time. It wasn't a matter of any one individual putting pressure on her. It was a matter of whether dating someone from work was a good idea. A different floor or department may not matter in the grand scheme of things. Victoria knew of several office romances that had failed to get off the ground or ended before they resulted in anything meaningful. However, all indications said that Thomas was a different kind of person. His level of sincerity was something that couldn't be faked or dismissed.

Thomas and Victoria got together on several other occasions. It didn't matter if it was for lunch, dinner or simply going out after work for a drink. It was all a celebration toward a new beginning for Victoria and it felt right. But there were other issues to consider outside of her emotional house. Chiefly, Jasmine and her parents. Their opinions were vital when it came to taking her relationship with Thomas to the next level so to speak. But if that meant waiting a week, a month or even longer then so be it.

Victoria arrived at her parents' home just before three-thirty. Jasmine was in the kitchen working on a glass of milk and a slice of chocolate cake. Making the snack all the more enjoyable was the fact that she didn't have school...or homework.

Gayle was standing over the sink rinsing suds from the dishes she was had washed. Dad was probably somewhere around the house doing whatever. It was a warm and sunny afternoon so he was probably in the backyard working in the garden. He was especially proud of the hydrangea and azalea bushes that he had planted years ago. The hydrangeas grew to be over five feet tall. When they bloomed, the lavender colored sprouts against the dark green leaves were magnificent. If nothing else, dad had one hell of a green thumb.

Smeared across Jasmine's lips was a thin layer of chocolate frosting which Victoria thought looked kind of cute and messy at the same time. It said that she was thoroughly enjoying herself.

"What's going on mom?" Victoria asked.

"You're early. I didn't expect to see you so soon," Gayle said after giving her daughter a light kiss on the left cheek.

"It's such a beautiful day outside I decided to take the afternoon off. Since I couldn't take a mental health day this was the next best thing," Victoria said in a humorous manner. "Mother Nature sure came through for me," she added.

"Worth it?" Gayle asked.

"And then some. I should've considered doing this a long time ago. It felt good to get out of the office and enjoy the day. Between the two of us, I could really get used to this. Where's dad?" Victoria asked.

"He was in the backyard a little while ago with his girlfriend Ms. Hydrangea," Gayle said as she turned her head to the left and then the right to get a better view out of the window. "I don't see him, so he may have gone upstairs," she added.

"Either way, I'm sure he's doing just fine," Victoria said.

Gayle didn't add anything more to the conversation. Her focus returned to the dishes in the sink. She didn't respond to Victoria calling her name either. It was not until she was tapped on the shoulder did Gayle snap out of her momentary daze.

"Mom, are you okay?" Victoria asked.

"Oh, I'm fine. Just a little tired. I haven't been getting much sleep, that's all," Gayle responded.

"Does this have anything to do with dad?" Victoria asked. She hoped her mother would open up. There had been too many times where she kept important information about dad bottled up inside.

"Maybe a little bit. But we'll talk about that later," Gayle said. After drying her hands, she wiped her eyes. They were noticeably red and slightly moist.

Victoria could see from the expression on her mother's face that there was more to the story than she was telling. Perhaps she was holding back since Jasmine was close by.

Jasmine was still focused on the goodies in front of her. However, Victoria was sure that she was taking in every word and processing those words the best way she could. Especially when it involved her grandfather.

Victoria had to get Jasmine out of the kitchen without raising her curiosity any further. All things being considered, Victoria decided to take the direct route. It worked in the past.

"Jasmine why don't you go into the living room and watch television. Grandma and I have to talk about something very important," Victoria said. Her tone was even and measured. If Jasmine were to pick up on anything, Victoria believed that was simply the cost of doing business and maintaining a high level of privacy.

With Jasmine out of the way Victoria took the opportunity to confront her mother once again; but not in an adversarial manner.

"All right mom lets have it." Victoria began. Her tone said that it was time to unpack the truth and get to the bottom of the situation about dad.

Gayle rinsed and placed the last glass in the draining tray adjacent to the sink. She dried her moist hands on the towel that hung on the door of the cabinet below. Gayle couldn't look Victoria in the eye as she turned away from the sink. Her movements were stiff and hesitant as if she were being led to her last meal accompanied by the prison's warden and a priest.

Not wanting Wesley to suddenly appear in the middle of their "talk," Gayle steered Victoria toward the French doors which led to the backyard.

It was difficult for her to explain things to Wesley when he finally came around. Having to speak to her daughter would only bring back the emotional turmoil that she had gone through. Whether she liked it or not, she had to relive the nightmare all over again. There was no way around it. She needed to and had to open up to someone close. Someone who's opinion she valued and trusted.

Gayle walked toward the middle of the yard barely having the energy to place one foot in front of the other. She moved across the freshly manicured grass as if she were alone in the world despite having her daughter at her side. Gayle wondered how she would describe someone that had raised, taught and comforted Victoria in the past was no longer that person. More importantly, Gayle wondered how Victoria would take the news. In either scenario Gayle felt trapped as being the bearer of bad news.

Gayle could see Victoria had some idea that something awful had happened or was about to happen. It was also abundantly clear that either situation involved her father. This was no time to indulge in some sort of guessing game.

Out with it Gayle secretly chastised herself.

The intensity of the sun did little to suppress the chill that Gayle felt inside as she began to tell her story. Mercifully as she spoke, Gayle began to feel the weight of the world loosen its grip on her physical and emotional being. At the same time Gayle said a silent prayer of thanks that her daughter was able to be with her. The role of comfort provider was reversed between mother and daughter. Gayle had no problem with that at all.

As Wesley descended the stairs his mind tried to process his actions as described by Gayle. But at the same time, it had to have been some kind of terrible mistake. That or was he recalling some mind-bending dream. Gayle said something about him not being in control of his mental facilities. That was impossible. As far as he knew there was no history of mental illness on his side of the family. His parents both died of natural causes. His brother was as fit as ever. At forty-seven he ran the marathon and topped his personal best time from the year before. Good health from top to bottom ran in his genes. But Gayle was so sure in her convictions. She wouldn't make up such a horrible story about him under any circumstances. She was not that kind of person even on her worst day.

As ugly as the description which Gayle laid out appeared to be, somewhere in the dark whispers of his mind Wesley had to consider the possibility that her words maybe true. Could it be that he was in fact losing his mind to a disease that may eventually take him away from his family?

Wesley believed that family meant everything. Family provided a sense of serenity and balance in an otherwise turbulent and confusing world. Family would tell the story of how a person treated their fellow man. Be it with kindness and compassion or with total indifference. Again, Wesley held that if it weren't for the love and support of family, life itself would be meaningless.

Wesley stopped in his tracks to watch Jasmine sitting on the couch in front of the television. The cartoon she was taking in told the story of a fish trying to convince its captor that there were bigger and better meals in the sea. Jasmine squealed with delight as man and fish each stated their case. One for survival, the other for hunger. Wesley didn't have the heart to disturb her.

Wesley turned toward the kitchen hoping to find Gayle. He needed to speak with her about what she said had occurred. However much to his disappointment she was nowhere to be found. Wesley went over to the refrigerator and examined the contents inside. He reached for his first can of beer in more than two weeks. It wasn't as if he didn't enjoy the taste he had to be in the right mood at the right time. Wesley walked over to the sink and looked out the window where he caught a glimpse of Gayle and much to his surprise Victoria. They appeared to be having one of those mother and daughter talks that Gayle spoke about. Wesley certainly didn't want to interfere in a place where he didn't necessarily belong. A light smile creased his face followed by a long swallow of his beverage. As far as Victoria, he would speak with her later.

After finishing his beer Wesley figured he needed some of that "alone time" that everyone spoke about. Besides for whatever it was worth now was as good a time as any to sort through things on his own. A self-evaluation without the high cost of a professional Wesley teased himself.

Wesley searched his pockets for his keys. After finding them he left the house.

When Gayle and Victoria came back inside, they heard the sound of the television unsure if Jasmine was still awake. Victoria walked into the living room and found that Jasmine was out for the count and appeared to have been that way for some time. She wondered if dad were around. He wouldn't leave without saying something unless he was having one of those episodes' mom spoke about.

"Mom, I don't think dad is home," Victoria said. Her voice had a tone of worry. "Jasmine is on the couch asleep," she added.

"Did you check upstairs?" Gayle asked.

"No. But don't you think he would have come down by now after hearing our voices? Victoria responded to her mother's question.

"True. But I'll go up and check anyway," Gayle offered.

Victoria was unsure what to make of the current situation. Should she accompany her mother upstairs or wait until she got back? Perhaps she was making a mountain out of a mole hill so to speak. There was no concrete evidence to conclude that anything was wrong. Dad had every right to go out on his own if he felt like it.

Victoria turned her attention back to Jasmine while she waited for her mother's return. Jasmine was still comfortably asleep.

"Well, you were right he's not here. I wonder where he could have gone?" Gayle asked mildly irritated.

"Do you think dad's disappearance had anything to do with what happened?"

Gayle had no response for her daughter. But if she knew her husband the way she was sure that she had, the answer to Victoria's question was a resounding yes. Gayle was sure Wesley was hiding the wave of confusion that he must have felt. While Gayle didn't expect Wesley to fly off in a wild range, there was an odd calmness about his demeanor that she had not expected when the dust settled.

Victoria didn't want to seem overly concerned about her dad's whereabouts but she couldn't ignore the fact that for all intents and purposes he was missing.

However, all fears were put to rest when Wesley walked through the front door with an overflowing shopping bag in his hands and a beaming smile on his face.

Between Gayle and Victoria, it didn't seem fair to bring up accusations of a decaying mind to the man that they both loved so much. That conversation could be had at another time and on another day.

"Let me give you a hand with that dad," Victoria offered.

"That's my girl," Wesley said still beaming from ear to ear.

Almost four months had come and gone since Victoria had that heart to heart with her mother concerning her dad's health. During that time thoughts of her parents continued to surface no matter how much she tried to downplay her level of concern. However, Victoria made a point to speak with her mother at least twice a week to stay in the loop. As much as she tried to fish for any new information about dad, mom did her best in steering the conversation toward Victoria's life. Perhaps she believed that not focusing on dad's mental health on a daily basis helped to keep her mentally afloat. Mom had confessed that for the most part dad was his usual self. He complained some, she still had to pick up after him at times and he loved her very much. Mom said it was a lot of simple things that dad hadn't lost. He would always kiss her at night before they slept and would kiss her the next morning. He even got behind the sink and washed the dishes every now and then when mom was tired. And flowers mom revealed. Flowers were a big part of dad doing loving things like he'd done in the past.

Victoria made mom promise that she would not hesitate to call at any time of the day or night if and when things got bad.

Victoria hated being away from the city and the past two days felt like an eternity. When she spoke to her mother earlier, there was an overwhelming sense that something was not right. It was a way mom spoke which did not sit well.

As the plane finally touched down Victoria hoped wouldn't have to wait a ridiculous amount of time for her luggage to appear on the carousel. As luck would have it within fifteen minutes Victoria had her suitcase in hand and was directed to the taxi stand outside. There were several unoccupied vehicles waiting for a potential fare. Victoria pulled the passenger side door open and entered the first car in line. She eased her tired frame onto the soft leather seat and stared out the side window as the vehicle pulled away from the airport. She had no intention of engaging in conversation. Victoria's thoughts were of reaching her parent's house as soon as possible. Her thoughts focused not only on seeing mom and dad, but Jasmine as well.

Mercifully there was very little traffic on the parkway and the taxi breezed along at a steady fifty-five miles an hour. However, Victoria mentally pushed the speed to sixty.

As if in tune with Victoria's thoughts of wanting to be left alone the driver kept his mind on the traffic ahead. Occasionally he responded to someone on the other end of communication device tucked securely in his right ear. The driver spoke in his native tongue and his head bobbed up and down in response to the comments coming from the other end of the call.

Every now and then the driver would switch from speaking Spanish to English. Although Victoria was not fluent with the language, she managed to pick up on a word or phrase here and there. The driver was complaining about having to put in a double shift last week just to break even. He was also upset that his wife hadn't fixed dinner for him in three days and he was left to fend for himself. When he switched back to English, he said something about spending more time with his girlfriend who lived in the Bronx. The driver tried to lower his voice but Victoria heard enough to see that this guy was a total low life. The person on the other end must have said something hilarious causing the driver to burst out in laughter as if he were in a bar where the high volume of noise was acceptable.

Victoria guessed that his wife was probably a hard-working woman. She may not have a job to report to everyday, but spent most of her time taking care of this ungrateful asshole while keeping a descent home. Victoria got the sense that no matter how well things may be going for this guy he would find time to bitch and moan about something.

Victoria decided that she was wasting valuable time thinking about the life of a stranger especially when there was nothing she could do about it. Victoria changed mental gears and began to focus on her own situation.

Thirty minutes later Victoria was standing at the front door of her parent's house. She looked up at the sky and took note of the dark gray clouds rolling in overhead. Victoria was glad that the bad weather hadn't started yet. She hated flying or driving in threatening weather.

When Victoria entered the house, she noticed that it was oddly quiet. She took that as a bad sign. Involuntarily Victoria tightened her grip on the handle of her suitcase. She called out for her parents and then Jasmine, but there was no response.

As she entered the kitchen Victoria's vision locked on a note attached to the door of the refrigerator. It was held in place by a flowered magnet. Undoubtedly it would explain why the house was deserted. As she began reading, Victoria had some difficulty in making it through the third line before her heart began to accelerate.

Dad was in the hospital.

As Victoria held the note in her unsteady hand, she experienced some difficulty in focusing on the rest of the message. The note fell to the kitchen floor. Although there was no sound it may as well have been a ton of bricks that Victoria previously held in her hand. Victoria felt as if she had been punched in the gut by a professional fighter and she was on the losing end of a twelve-round fight.

After Victoria managed to gather her thoughts, she fished around in her pocketbook and pulled out her cell phone. She scrolled through her list of contacts and pressed the call button hoping that her mother would answer. Most hospitals didn't allow the use of cell phones within its confines but this was an emergency. Most people paid little attention to the restriction unless they were interrupted by security or the hospital's staff.

"Mom," Victoria began.

"Is everything all right? What about dad? Is Jasmine okay?" Victoria's questions were delivered in rapid fire succession which gave Gayle very little opportunity to respond.

"The doctors are with him now," Gayle said. Although her voice was barely audible Victoria was able to understand her words, as frightening as they were.

"He had another attack," Gayle said. "This one was much worse than the one he suffered a few months ago."

Victoria could hear the sound of fear in her mother's voice which added to her own level of apprehension. She recalled having to work on her mother before she revealed anything about dad's prior heart attack which was mild according to the doctors.

Victoria's thoughts turned to Jasmine and what she must be going through right now. Sadly, Jasmine was living through the same crisis as everyone else in spite of the wall of protection they tried to build around her. In a child's mind the entire episode had to be frightening. The thought of her seeing the only male hero in her life laid out on a stretcher, being wheeled out of grandma's house…

Victoria stopped before she completed her thought.

"Where's Jasmine?" Victoria asked.

"She's right here with me," Gayle whispered.

"Mom, I know you can't get into any specifics right now but can you at least tell me what happened?" Victoria asked.

"Everything was going fine until yesterday afternoon. We made plans that morning to go out for lunch and that's when it happened. Wesley began acting strange as if he had no idea of his surroundings or . . ." Gayle hesitated choking back her words as an emotion of fear took hold.

Gayle immediately recovered and was able to continue speaking.

"I was in the den when I heard this terrible noise coming from the living room. By the time I got there your father was on the floor clutching his chest writhing in pain. I've never heard your father scream that loud before. Thank the good Lord that I was in the next room." Gayle was not sure that she could continue. However, she found the inner strength to go on.

"I called 9-1-1 and the operator told me exactly what to do until EMS arrived. Bless her soul because to tell you the truth, I don't believe I could have gotten this far without her help. The paramedics got here within fifteen minutes of my call and they began working on your father. They were able to get him stabilized and ready for transport while I stood there helpless," Gayle said in a defeated tone. This time she could not hold back the stream of tears. She turned her shoulder away from Jasmine and wiped her cheeks.

"Mom, you can't blame yourself. You did everything humanly possible under the circumstances. Because you were there dad's chances of getting past this increased a thousand-fold. Mom you're the strongest woman I know. Without a doubt you proved that today. Like I said, you did everything possible." The idea that mom should be awarded the badge of courage ran through Victoria's mind.

There were a few moments of silence between the women which seemed to hang in the air longer than expected.

But then Gayle spoke up.

"I did my best to keep Jasmine out of the way. But you know your daughter. She has a curious mind, is sharp as a tack and can see when adults are trying to hide things from her. I promise Vicky, I really tried. I did everything I could to keep her out of the way while they worked on your father Gayle repeated. I have to tell you Vicky, Jasmine was one brave little girl," Gayle complimented.

"That being said. I know when a child needs the comfort only a mother can supply. Jasmine had that look in her eye today," Gayle offered based on her years of experience as a parent herself.

In the background Victoria could hear the sound of the hospital's intercom calling out the name of one physician or the other asking them to dial an extension or report to a specific area within the structure.

"How is Jasmine doing now?" Victoria asked.

"She seems to be much better now. At least that's how it appears to be on the outside. You know better than anyone that Jasmine has a tendency to hide her feelings and sometimes it's difficult to get her to open up."

Victoria could have easily jumped on that personality trait with her mother but decided to let it go.

"Mom, I'll be there as quickly as I can," Victoria said. Although her voice seemed strong and unwavering Victoria was just as frightened as her mother.

The sight of dad being in the hospital with tubes attached to his body tore at Victoria's core. As impossible as it was to understand Victoria had a short-lived vision of Raymond in the hospital during his final days.

When she looked up Gayle noticed two doctors heading in her

direction. In her mind they appeared to be moving in slow motion. Their knee length unbuttoned white coats flapped gently in the breeze as they drew closer. Gayle's inner feelings said that the news was not going to be positive. The elder physician held a clipboard in his hand. He ran the fingers of his right hand through the salt and pepper hair on his head as if puzzled by some complex medical issue. Could it have been about her husband Gayle wondered? She clenched her fists feeling a sense of overwhelming dread. However, it could have just as easily been some other patient having nothing to do with her family.

The elder physician appeared to be explaining something to his colleague. Gayle could see his lips moving but heard no sound as he jabbed at the paperwork for emphasis. Gayle listened as the echo of their heels made contact with the polished floor. The physicians walked side by side as if they were military officials about to deliver marching orders to the troops.

If the doctors had attended to Wesley, Gayle didn't want to hear anything they had to say other than giving Wesley a clean bill of health stating that he can be discharged in the morning. If only she could click her heels and have a magical moment of her own. Maybe she should innocently turn her back on the approaching doctors and pretend they were looking for someone else.

Gayle was alone once again to bear the stinging force of the doctor's message. Although Gayle knew Victoria was on her way that knowledge failed to help her at the moment. Privately Gayle was not sure how much she could take. Being an emotionally strong person required a mindset that Gayle was not sure she possessed any longer. In spite of the battles that she had won in the past, Gayle's feeling of self-doubt could not be ignored. In the end Gayle understood that she was not thinking clearly. She said a silent prayer seeking guidance and strength from her heavenly Father. Her prayers were answered in the form of her daughter's appearance.

Without using all of the medical terms that the doctors bombarded her with Gayle revealed everything she could remember about Wesley's condition. The doctors wanted to keep him for a few days. They said something about having to run additional tests on him.

Their concern had to do with Wesley's advanced age and how his system would process the medication they had to administer. Both doctors said there was a small possibility that Wesley's system may attempt to reject the very same medication that was given to help him. They said that only time would tell. But they were optimistic toward a positive outcome.

Victoria could see the obvious pain registered on her mother's face as she spoke. She understood that mom was under pressure but the sense of resignation in her voice was nothing like the woman she had known.

"Was dad still sleeping the last time you checked on him?" Victoria inquired.

"His doctor said that he would be out for the next several hours and perhaps through the night. But you can go up and see him if you want too. His room is on the third floor. Room three twenty-four. I'll wait here with Jasmine," Gayle concluded as she lightly touched the child's arm.

Something in Victoria caused her to momentarily hesitate. She didn't know which direction would provide the quickest and safest alley of escape. This could not really be happening. Should she turn left toward the exit sign with Jasmine in tow, or toward the bank of elevators that would take her to her dad's room?

The correct decision immediately surfaced and was implemented.

While walking down the hallway toward her father's room, Victoria questioned her feelings. She could not control the chill that tickled her insides. Hearing about the reason that put dad in the hospital was one thing. However, having to actually see him in such a vulnerable state was an entirely different matter. Victoria had the strength to counsel her mother and bear some of her pain. But on the other side, who was there to rescue her when she needed a lifeline thrown in her direction.

Victoria was not looking to open herself to some stranger on a crisis hotline. At this moment Victoria wanted to reach out and touch a warm bodied individual and unburden her soul. There had to be someone who would welcome her with open arms and take her to a place of comfort.

There had to be.

It was not until Victoria entered her father's room did she come to fully understand and appreciate the emotion called fear. She had come to realize firsthand the power the sentiment had at its disposal and the havoc it can wield.

Victoria watched her father lying in bed surrounded by machines monitoring his vital signs. His chest rose and fell as he breathed. There were tubes attached to his arms, sensors attached to his chest and an oxygen mask covering his mouth.

According to mom the paramedics had to jump start dad's heart several times before getting a stable rhythm. The doctors were concerned with dad's shallow breathing and his irregular heartbeat. This became an issue a second time shortly after he was admitted.

Victoria stood at the foot of the bed watching. Dad seemed unrecognizable. If it weren't for the two-inch scar above his right eye, Victoria could have made an argument that she'd entered the wrong room. However, the scar above his right eye was a constant reminder that he should have left renovating the basement ceiling to a professional contractor.

A wave of their history together flooded Victoria's mind. Dad taught her how to tie her shoes. He would read a story to her on most nights before she fell asleep. Dad was the one that bought her first pair of skates and it was dad who taught her how to ride a bicycle. Lastly and more importantly, dad was there when she experienced her first crush. He explained how young boys thought. As a young girl she understood parts of what dad said that made them tick but on others, boys seemed downright alien. The situation brought a slight smile to her face as she now looked down on her father. Victoria wanted to scream out his name and demand that he get up and be the man that he used to be.

That wasn't too much to ask.

Her voice was barely above a whisper when she addressed the figure laying before her. Victoria spoke to the individual not as a patient, but as her father.

"Wake up daddy it's me Vicky." Her voice was almost childlike.

"Can't you hear me daddy?"

Victoria pulled over a chair and placed it beside the bed. She slowly eased her body down onto the seat and then lightly touched her father's warm hand. In spite of the intravenous tubes Victoria carefully raised her father's hand to her lips and gently planted a kiss. It was as if there were some truth to the tale about a princess kissing a toad and a handsome prince would appear.

Victoria then thought about the supposed power of prayer and everything she had heard that it could do. Whether she believed in it or not, now was not the time to question what so many held to be true.

Victoria clasped her hands tightly together and bowed her head. She began her offering with the Lord's Prayer. As she prayed Victoria's lips began to tremble slightly. But she did not try and stop their movement. Perhaps the fact that she made an attempt at prayer may garner her some favor with the deity above. Maybe it wasn't what was said that made all the difference in the world. What if it was all about the level of sincerity which fueled an answer? Victoria spoke the first words that came to mind and directly from her heart.

"Where's mom?" Jasmine asked after twenty minutes had passed.

"She's still upstairs with grandpa, but she should be back any minute." Gayle wasn't sure if her answer would satisfy Jasmine's curiosity, but judging by her silence it seemed to have worked.

Thinking of Jasmine's inquiry, Gayle herself wondered what was taking Victoria so long. Wesley was sedated and expected to be out for the night. So what in the world could she be doing?

Victoria realized that there was nothing more she could say or do tonight. She would pick up mom tomorrow morning and come back to the hospital for any updates on dad's condition. Perhaps the situation would have changed for the better.

Gayle and Victoria would have liked to stay a while longer but the intercom stated that visiting hours would be ending in fifteen minutes.

Victoria offered to stay with her mother at her place overnight, but Gayle insisted that she was fine and would see them in the morning. In spite of Victoria pressing the issue Gayle stood firm in her decision.

"Go home and take care of your daughter. I'll be fine," Gayle said.

Victoria gave in.

Good nights and hugs all around.

During the ride home Jasmine couldn't stop talking. Perhaps it was her way of expressing an inner fear about her grandfather. Each time she asked a question Victoria put her off by telling Jasmine to ask her grandmother.

"But grandma told me to ask you when we got home," Jasmine responded through a tone of frustration.

"Well we're not home yet are we," Victoria snapped. However, she immediately felt bad for taking out her frustration on an innocent child. She offered a sincere apology promising that they would discuss things later.

After seeing that Jasmine had dinner and bathed, Victoria secured her second wind. She settled into her bedroom with a cup of tea in hand and dialed her mother's number.

Gayle answered on the third ring.

"Hi mom," Victoria began.

"How are you feeling? I know you've got to be tired but I wanted to check on you."

"I'm okay thank God. I never imagined something like this would have happened. I had a hard time recognizing your father at one point. When the heart attacked started your father's face twisted and contorted beyond his control. The pain must have been unbearable. This was nothing like the first time which was mild by comparison. I should have saw the signs. I should have," Gayle repeated. "But God forgive me I missed it."

"Mom, like I said before you can't continue to blame yourself for what happened. There's no sense in beating yourself up. At the time you did everything possible," Victoria said in a soothing yet firm tone. It was important that she reassure her mother that anyone would have reacted the same way and that she did nothing wrong."

"Mom what happened just before the attack happened?" Victoria asked.

"I don't remember," Gayle said without hesitation.

"Think about it mom. What were you and dad talking about?"

Gayle searched her mind as far back as she could before responding.

"It wasn't anything special. We could have been talking about the weather for all I know," Gayle said in a frivolous sort of way.

"Mom this is serious," Victoria said hoping to jog her mother's memory.

"You have to try harder. It will come. Trust me," Victoria pressed.

Just as Victoria said, Gayle repeated everything that happened to the best of her recollection. There were a few things that she added which were omitted earlier believing they were not relevant.

There was a sadness in Gayle's voice that seemed to resonate through the telephone line and physically touch Victoria. It was difficult enough hearing mom speak about dad with such a morbid sense of resignation.

"Mom don't give up," Victoria said. However, she immediately realized that was a poor choice of words and wished she could take it back.

"How can you say something like that? Giving up is not an option,"

Gayle snapped back in response. The sorrow that was previously evident in her voice was replaced with an anger directed at Victoria.

"I'm sorry mom. I didn't mean that at all. I'm just trying to understand the situation," Victoria said.

"The situation is simple. We have to rally around your father because he's going to need every ounce of our support and energy. We also need to leave things in God's capable hands and pray for the best," Gayle said.

Victoria was glad to see that mom's demeanor had changed and that the anger she displayed had disappeared but perhaps not necessarily forgotten.

Gayle reverted to the woman Victoria had known most of her life. Resilient and as strong willed as ever.

Usually, Victoria's emotions leaned toward the logical versus the spiritual when it came to understanding and rectifying difficult situations. Yet in this case, based on her mother's view she had very little choice because in the end the power of prayer was the only solution.

"Okay mom. What about tomorrow?" Victoria asked.

"What do you mean?" Gayle responded in a puzzled manner.

"What time should I pick you up? Victoria asked.

"What about Jasmine. Are you going to let her go to school?" Gayle asked once she recovered.

"I was thinking about keeping her at home and allowing her to come with us to see dad. But when I thought about it, I decided that was not a good idea. Right now, I think she needs the socialization of her friends to act as her crutch to help her emotionally. I'll put her on the bus as usual and pick you up around nine o'clock or so. How does that sound?" Victoria asked.

"Perfect. Now let me get some sleep," Gayle said in a humorous manner.

"I love you mom."

"I love you too honey."

As mother and daughter stepped off the elevator on the third floor Gayle noticed Wesley's doctor at the nurse's station. When his conversation ended the doctor turned in their direction realizing that they may want to speak with him.

"Good morning," the doctor began with his hand extended. "You may recall that we met briefly last night."

"Yes, I do. Good morning doctor," Gayle responded. "This is my daughter Victoria."

The doctor smiled and also shook Victoria's right hand.

Victoria appreciated the gesture but she wanted to get right to the point.

"Doctor, would you mind giving us an update on my father's condition," she began.

The doctor looked down and turned to the second page of the patient medical chart in his hand.

"Let's go to my office where we can speak comfortably," the doctor suggested.

The doctor's office was around the corner from the nurse's station. The space had the look and feel of a Wall Street executive's office and nothing like that of a physician. Everything appeared to be in its proper place. Nothing seemed out of order from the pens and pencils that lay on the massive oak desk, to the books and medical journals on the shelves. There were a fair number of framed awards on the walls ranging from several years ago to the present.

As they sat in the chairs facing the doctor Gayle was glad that Victoria took the lead when seeking information about her father's condition. Gayle conceded that contrary to her brave front she was grateful for Victoria's company.

"Yesterday you mentioned something about running additional tests on my father and the possibility that his system may reject the medication he is being given. Can you give us more information doctor?" Victoria asked.

"Right. I see that your father recently celebrated his seventy-fifth birthday. Congratulations. However, the downside that comes with aging is that certain parts of our bodies fail to function as efficiently as they had in the past. I'm sure you both understand that as a part of living. I believe that's happening here. I see that your father has had trouble in the past with an elevated blood sugar issue. Has he spoken with his endocrinologist about that?"

Victoria responded that they had and Wesley has been put on a strict diet to help lower his blood sugar level.

The doctor turned his attention away from Victoria for the moment and focused on Gayle.

"At the moment your husband is still asleep, but I've scheduled him for a CT scan at eleven-thirty this morning and hopefully when the tests results come back, we'll know more."

"A CT scan?" Gayle repeated. "What do you expect to find?"

"Considering the two episodes that your husband experienced, the second of which resulted in his hospitalization there's a distinct possibility that one or more of his arteries may be causing a reduced flow of blood to his heart. Are either of you familiar with the term Atherosclerosis?" the doctor asked.

Both Gayle and Victoria stated that they had, but were unaware of the in-depth specifics of the condition. The doctor explained the symptoms and the procedure to resolve the issue in an effort to have the patient return to their normal living activities. His explanation included the possibility of dad having to undergo coronary artery bypass surgery.

With the possibility of surgery looming, Gayle unknowingly squeezed Victoria's hand which was accompanied by a low gasp. As Victoria listened to the doctor speak, she formed a distinct dislike for the man as a person. Perhaps it was the matter-of-fact tone that he used when speaking, which for her appeared to be void of any emotion. His words almost seemed rehearsed if not mechanical. However, no matter how she felt on the inside Victoria had to remain focused and concentrate on what was being said.

Victoria looked to the clock that hung on the wall to the right of the doctor's desk. Ten-fifteen.

Victoria wondered if dad were awake and alert by now or if the nurse had to wake him up for the scheduled procedure.

Gayle regained her composure and listened intently to the doctor's words. He explained what they would be looking for once the CT scan was complete. Her expression twisted slightly at the idea of Wesley being treated as some sort of medical specimen. The fact that further testing was necessary for his overall care meant very little to her at the moment.

"I think it's time that I check on my husband," Gayle said. She wanted to get away from the doctor's presence as quick as possible. Gayle was unsure if Victoria felt the same way, but there was something about the doctor's manner that left a bad feeling in the pit of her stomach.

"That's a good idea. Hopefully he's awake by now. Let me walk you back to the nurses' station," the doctor offered.

Wesley's eyes slowly opened but he was still unable to focus on his surroundings. There was an oxygen mask strapped to his face which added to his sense of confusion. Wesley attempted to raise his arm but found it was restricted by an intravenous tube. He looked up and noticed a half a bag of saline solution hanging from a pole. There was a needle taped into place on the top of his hand just above his knuckles.

Wesley couldn't remember for the life of him how or why he woke up in the hospital of all places. Wesley ran his left hand under his chin and felt the slight growth of hair. In addition to the how and why of it all Wesley wanted to know how long he'd been here.

Just as Wesley completed the puzzling question to himself an orderly entered the room.

"Ah. You're finally awake. You slept right through the night. You gave us quite a scare for a minute. You have a big day ahead of you. How are you feeling?" The woman's comments and question were delivered in rapid fire succession as if breathing was an afterthought.

She moved around the room with the speed of a wind-up doll. Adjusting the blinds, smoothing out the sheets and blankets on the bed.

"Oh, by the way," she paused momentarily. "Your wife and daughter are on their way up to see you. They can't stay long because you're scheduled for a CT scan this morning. The doctor will also stop by and answer any questions you may have. Also, someone from radiology will be here to take you upstairs for the scan."

There she went again. Wesley humorously thought about lending her the oxygen mask attached to his face. Clearly, she needed it more than he did.

With that being said the orderly departed leaving Wesley with no chance to ask what the hell was going on. A damn CT scan, what was that all about? Wesley admitted that he had a slight headache but was a CT scan necessary. There had to be more to it considering the morning he was having so far.

Wesley couldn't wait to see and speak with Gayle and Victoria. Perhaps they could clear up the thousand or so questions he had. The fact that Victoria was here made the morning all the more surreal. She should be at work instead of roaming the halls of the hospital to see her old man.

Gayle and Victoria entered the room.

"Well, well, well," Wesley offered in a sardonic manner.

"I see the reinforcements have arrived." Whether he realized it or not there was a look of relief on his face at the sight of familiar faces in spite of his comments.

"Good morning to you too," Gayle responded with a slight jab of her own. At least on the outside Wesley seemed like his old ornery self. This was something that Gayle took as a measure of comfort in spite of everything happening… and the events to come.

"Hey dad," Victoria said as she approached the side of the bed. She planted a light kiss on his cheek when what she really wanted to do was to grab and hold him tight.

Wesley had a barrage of questions waiting on the tip of his tongue but he wanted to get away from the hospital first.

"I hope you guys bought my clothes. I'm ready to get out of here," Wesley announced to his wife and daughter and anyone else within the range of his voice.

"Yes, I have your clothes, but we're not ready to leave just yet," Gayle said. She turned her head and looked at Victoria who remained silent.

"What do you mean by that?" Wesley asked.

"Wesley there's something we have to talk about," Gayle began.

"I'm sure the doctor told you about the blockage in your artery that has to be addressed. Right?"

Wesley sank back into the pillow revealing a clear sign of the disappointment he felt at the prospect of having surgery. An important procedure he understood, but surgery just the same.

Gayle said something called a coronary CT angiogram was required to determine how much of a blockage is interrupting the flow of blood to his heart.

"This is why you had the second heart attack. The first one was kind of a warning shot. I know, it scared the both of us but now we have to do something about it before things get worse," Gayle said.

Wesley heard the words coming from his wife and she was right about the first attack. Wesley recalled the exact time that it happened. In hindsight, Wesley wished he had been more forthcoming and opened up to Gayle over the past few months. But now was not the time for feeling sorry for himself. This was a time for decision making and taking responsibility for his health. If that meant putting things, important things in the hands of the doctors, he had very little choice in the matter.

Thomas had no idea where he stood with Victoria from a relationship standpoint. Over the past two weeks she appeared to have been as distant as the moon itself. Although he managed to get in a conversation here and there it was nothing substantial. Other than that, she was either out of the office, in a meeting or traveling on business. He was ready to reach out to someone in Victoria's office hoping they might have some insight about what was going on. Thomas knew Victoria and Sharon were close so perhaps she may have confided in her.

He and Sharon had similar views on a variety of subjects and she was a good friend. With that Thomas felt he wouldn't be stepping out of bounds by asking about Victoria. Thomas felt strong enough about his feelings toward Victoria to take that chance. If it blew up in his face then so be it.

It didn't take a rocket scientist to see that there was something going on that had Victoria tied up in knots. On the rare occasions that he had the opportunity to speak with her she seemed preoccupied or at the very least distracted.

The last few weeks had been time well forgotten as far as Victoria was concerned. To make matters worse she had to come to terms with Thomas. She couldn't continue avoiding his company or chopping off their conversations as if she were not interested in him. Thomas turned out to be the best thing that had happened to her in a very long time and he did not deserve to be treated as an afterthought.

Victoria needed to make a concerted effort to change that. She had to make things right and lay her cards on the table to let Thomas know how she felt on the inside.

Gayle had all the reasons in the world to worry. It was just after one-thirty afternoon and Wesley hadn't gotten out of bed yet. In the past even on his worst day, he was usually up and about doing something. There was always some project that he felt compelled to work on. The project may not have turned out the way he had planned but he never believed in down time and would move on to something different. Gayle recalled last year when Wesley was battling the flu, he continued working in the garage on a wooden bench that he started. God bless his soul Gayle thought; the man didn't know when to stop.

Wesley refused Gayle's offer of lunch stating that he was not hungry. It didn't matter what was on the menu. Gayle decided that it was time to put her foot down and insist that he put something in his stomach. He had medication to take and she was not going to let him have it without eating something. She let him get away with that game yesterday but this was a new day and a different set of circumstances. Wesley began to become stronger and stronger each day. Gayle made a point to see that he stayed on the path toward a complete recovery. The surgery to clear his arteries were a success. His complaining about having to stay off his feet and in the hospital for two days post-surgery, fell on deaf ears. The doctors said that going forward Wesley would be fine as long as he stayed on the regiment of diet and exercise laid out for him. For her part, Gayle had no intention of allowing him to slip back into his old habits. If that meant reminding him every day then she was up to the task.

As time went by Victoria noticed that Jasmine was less and less inquisitive about her grandfather. There was no question that Jasmine loved her grandfather, but she was growing up and had issues and responsibilities of her own to tackle. Jasmine was involved with a dance group started by the music department at school, track and field practice on Saturday mornings and her all important social calendar. Jasmine was by no means the leader of the pack, but Victoria noticed that friends wanted her opinion on what television programs to watch, fashion do's and don'ts and what girl liked what boy and visa-versa. Victoria saw this as a positive sign and a necessary distraction for her daughter. Victoria also saw this as her daughter's inner strength shining through for everyone to see.

In spite of the whirlwind of activity that had taken place over the past few months, Victoria could no longer hide the fact that she wanted Thomas in her life more than she dared to confess. From a companion and emotional point of view shutting him out made no sense whatsoever. Victoria decided that she would open up about everything, from her dad's sickness, to Jasmine and her feeling toward him.

Tuesday morning just before eight o'clock, Gayle's eyes slowly opened as the blinding light from the sun spilled through the half-drawn blinds. Last night she forgot to pull the curtains together as she had usually done.

Gayle looked back at her husband and a smile creased her face. It had been a good night for Wesley who seemed to have slept with a sense of peace that she hadn't seen in quite a while. Moments later Wesley began to stir as if summoned by Gayle's inner thoughts.

"I haven't slept that well in weeks," Wesley said while reaching for the ceiling.

"I feel like I can take on the world this morning," he added.

"That may be true, but lets take it one step at a time okay champ. Remember you're not twenty-one anymore." Gayle said.

"Very funny," Wesley responded as he spun his feet out of the bed and onto the floor. He looked in Gayle's direction as he slid each one into his slippers.

"Do you have anything going on today?" Gayle called back from the bathroom.

"I can't think of a single thing," Wesley said happy that his schedule was clear.

"How about some breakfast?" Wesley asked.

"Sounds great. What are you going to fix?" Gayle asked. "I'm starved," she added.

"Oh, you're good. Wrong, but good," Wesley responded.

It was approaching one-thirty and Victoria had just ended a call with a potential client from San Francisco. The company, ZMTX Incorporated appeared to be on the outside looking in for several months and Victoria was not sure if she sealed the deal. Having them come on board with Real Time would further solidify their lead within the industry. However, Victoria worried about the cost and whether it would tarnish their reputation. Victoria had been directed to reach out to them in spite of her feelings to the contrary. The company had been embroiled in a copyright litigation just over two years ago. While litigation determined that no wrongdoing occurred on their part, the issue left an ugly stain as far as the advertising industry was concerned.

The President and CEO Thaddeus Wilburn spoke fast and loose with regard to the direction of the company from an advertising point of view. As Wilburn explained, they were small by industry standards but had great connections. Their senior staff were in discussions with other advertising agencies along the eastern corridor but no final decisions have been made. Apparently, the company was looking for the "right people" to spearhead an advertising campaign that would boost sales within a relatively short period of time.

As far as Victoria was concerned with an attitude like that, he may be looking for the right people for some time. Based on what she just heard, this may not be the right fit for Real Time. For Victoria it wasn't about the fast buck. One of the golden rules of the business related to word of mouth and positive exposure. It was not so much the idea of having flashing lights on a billboard above the city as it was about respect in the industry and dedication to its consumers. If ZMTX could not provide both, Victoria wanted no part of their business and she would put a voice to her opinion as far up the chain as were necessary.

Victoria turned her thoughts to matters that were inherently more to her liking. Specifically, dinner with Thomas. He called earlier in the day and wondered if she had any plans for the evening. Being the gentleman he was, Thomas apologized for calling on such short notice. However, Victoria would not have cared if it were three o'clock in the morning, it was good to hear his voice. With that in mind this was no time for beating around the bush with a false sense of indecision.

The problem was in finding someone to watch Jasmine. Victoria did not want to bother her mother feeling that she had enough on her plate. But it was early enough in the day to ask Sharon for a favor. Jasmine loved Sharon and they got along like two peas in a pod. Although Sharon had children of her own, she treated Jasmine as an additional member of her family without a second thought.

Victoria held her breath as she punched in Sharon's extension hoping for the best.

Twenty minutes later and as luck would have it Sharon agreed to come over and watch Jasmine for the evening.

"I knew the two of you would hit it off," Sharon said in a braggadocios kind of way. She also threw in an *'I told you so'* for good measure.

"Oh shut up," Victoria playfully and rapidly responded.

Hours later.

"I thought my cologne might have offended you," Thomas lightheartedly offered after they were seated. "You've been sort of distant lately."

"I'm really sorry it appeared that way. I've had some personal matters to deal with that's all," Victoria offered while intentionally steering clear of any specifics.

"As far as your cologne, I love it," Victoria said.

"Is there anything I can do to help? I'm a great listener when it counts," Thomas offered.

"It's nothing I can't handle. But thanks for asking," Victoria said while refusing to recall her conversation with Sharon where she pretty much bore her soul.

"I have no doubt that you can handle whatever it is, but have you considered letting someone help you? To be perfectly honest, I'd like to be that person. I understand that for all intents and purposes we've just met. But you're the person I've been looking forward to meeting for quite some time." Thomas took a moment to inhale and exhale before continuing.

"I'm sorry for being this forward but I'm a firm believer in saying what needs to be said, just as long as no one gets hurt in the process."

Thomas spoke with a sense of confidence and sincerity that it left Victoria stunned into silence and not knowing how to respond. It had been a lifetime ago since a man spoke to her with that level of passion. It was frightening yet exciting at the same time.

Over the years Victoria had become extremely guarded with her emotions which was probably why she chose to remain single. Certainly there was no rush in starting a relationship with anyone. However, with Thomas, it was something entirely different. There was something inviting about his personality that Victoria found irresistible.

"I'm not sure that I'm ready for something like this," was all that Victoria could manage following Thomas' revelation. The tone of her voice resembled someone attempting to stand on unsteady legs.

"Something like what? Thomas said as if seeking a deeper response from Victoria.

"There's nothing wrong with two people falling for each other. Life is meant to be unscripted Victoria. It's all about surprises and taking chances," Thomas continued.

"But you hardly know anything about me or my situation," Victoria responded directly.

Without thinking about what he was doing, Thomas reached for Victoria's hands as he spoke.

"I'm willing to learn everything there is to know about you no matter how long that takes. Victoria, I have strong feelings for you. I probably always have," Thomas said.

Victoria took time to study Thomas' face. She had no idea what she was searching for; perhaps a sign of deception? But she knew that was not possible. If anything, Victoria realized if she allowed herself a moment to let go, she would tell Thomas that her feelings for him were the same. She would tell him he entered her life at the right moment in time.

Instead.

"I could turn out to be your worst nightmare," Victoria offered as a matter of defense.

"I seriously doubt that. But that's a chance I'm willing to take," Thomas responded.

"And why is that?" Victoria asked feeling a slight chill run through her body.

Being here with Thomas was nothing like negotiating with a business rival or sitting across the table from a potential client. Hell, that was easy pickings and something she could handle in her sleep. But having to expose herself on an emotional level was altogether different. Real life. No takes.

Thomas smiled broadly and again rested his hands lightly on top of Victoria's as he spoke.

"The short answer is that I'm a glutton for punishment and I can walk over a bed of hot coals without flinching. Especially if the journey is worth the prize," Thomas responded.

"Victoria, I'm not asking you to make a decision right here and now. I want you to think about everything I've said. By no means am I a knight trying to sweep you off your feet. You stated that I didn't know anything about you. On a certain level you're absolutely correct. So to change that scenario I'm inviting you to tell me everything I need to know," Thomas said.

"I can't do that right now. Where would I begin?" Victoria said sincerely.

"If not now, then that gives me the chance to ask you out again," Thomas said thinking of the upside possibility.

"You've placed me in a very challenging position.

Congratulations," Victoria offered in somewhat of a complimentary manner.

"Well I do aim to please," Thomas quickly responded slightly bowing his head to one side in Victoria's direction.

Making the decision to dive in head first and test the waters, Victoria boldly responded.

"All right then how about this," Victoria said? Tomorrow night. Dinner at my house. Seven-thirty."

"With bells on lovely lady. With bells on," Thomas said with a tone of confidence in his voice.

"Oh don't be so sure of yourself mister. There's one other person that you have to impress and between you and me she's one tough cookie," Victoria responded warning Thomas about the challenge he was up against.

Dinner with Thomas was the breath of fresh air that Victoria had anticipated all day. Jasmine seemed to have taken to him from the very beginning. She was absolutely charming in a young girl sort of way. Yet mature enough to understand that she would be seeing more of Thomas as the weeks and months went by.

There were times during dinner where Jasmine made him blush and times where Thomas felt just slightly uncomfortable with her comments and questions. The upside however was that Jasmine's inquiries were never disrespectful. Thomas responded to her in a way that she could understand. He was never dismissive when considering Jasmine's age.

Much to Victoria's surprise Thomas was up to date on the latest video games, movies and text messaging lingo which were a big deal in Jasmine's peer group. Victoria continued to watch as Thomas interacted with Jasmine. At times he made her laugh out loud, but he also challenged her to see things from an adult's perspective.

As someone who lived their life in the age of technology, Thomas was surprisingly great with children leaving Victoria to wondered how and where he obtained his expertise. Victoria could now rightfully challenge Carole's opinion that eggheads were stiff and boring.

Thomas was anything but.

After clearing the table and cleaning up with Thomas' help, the pair took the opportunity to dive deeper into each other's life. They felt a sense of ease possibly because they were far from the public field of vision. Victoria's comfort level stemmed from the fact that she was at home and surrounded by all things familiar to her. Thomas, even if dropped into the middle of the ocean he would survive.

Thomas opened up about the loss of his sister and the affect it had on his family. He was five years old when it happened. His sister Deena had been warned on numerous occasions not to venture away from the house without adult supervision. But she never seemed to listen and usually did the opposite of what she was told. Thomas revealed that he witnessed the accident.

There was a ball rolling. A speeding truck. Then she was gone. She left the world as an innocent seven-year-old child.

"Who knew where her stubbornness may have taken her in this world," Thomas said.

There was an unmistakable sadness in Thomas' voice as he recalled that tragic event.

Thomas revealed that to this day he carried with him the last photo he and Deena had taken together. Thomas removed the photo from his wallet and gave it to Victoria.

It was Halloween. Deena was dressed as a fairy and he was outfitted as a pint-sized combat solider. From a back pack, a helmet and a toy rifle, Thomas had everything he needed for the part.

"I couldn't put that particular photo in an album if I tried. It just wouldn't seem right," Thomas said as though it would have been a mortal sin to do so.

"It was probably just as bad for your parents," Victoria responded as she handed the photo back to Thomas.

"You could say that. Divorced a year later, they blamed one another for what they perceived to have been the other's lack of supervision. My mother was in the kitchen and my father was in his home office going over work-related matters. My mother hated when he bought his work into the house. She felt that he neglected the family when that happened.

Once the litigation phase ended, my mother got the house, child support payments and me. My father got a thriving firm, a drinking problem and unsupervised visitation. Either way in the end, they moved on in different directions. Whether they're satisfied with their lives today, only they can speak to that," Thomas said.

Victoria couldn't help notice the change in Thomas' voice when he spoke about his parents. It was devoid of any warmth and he spoke in a monotone that could not be ignored. Victoria saw that version of Thomas as being light years away from the person she loved and respected.

"You seemed to have turned out just fine," Victoria began not knowing what else to say. But at least she speaking was truthfully.

"Thanks, but I still have my warts to keep in check," Thomas offered with a smile of confession pasted on his face. It was a clear attempt to lighten what could otherwise turn into a dark and depressing moment. He hadn't spoken to anyone about his parents in years, nor had he spoken to them in just as long.

"Where did you learn to cook like that?" Thomas asked.

"Everything was delicious."

"For the most part my mother taught me so many culinary tricks over the years. Also, meals seemed to have worked out during my trial-and-error phase. But mom, she can prepare a meal fit for a king's palace in no time flat. In the kitchen, she's second to none," Victoria bragged.

"I guess you've taken her lessons to heart since I just witnessed how much Jasmine enjoyed your cooking. If it's one thing I've learned is until children master an acquired taste, a meal is either going to be very good or very bad. As far as they're concerned there's only black or white without any gray areas to confuse their taste buds," Thomas said.

"Hey come to think of it, I owe you a night out don't I?" Victoria asked.

"I may let you off the hook on that offer," Thomas said.

A puzzled expression appeared on Victoria's face. She was unsure where Thomas was going with his statement.

"You keep cooking like that and I may never eat out again," Thomas said. "Interested in a position as a culinary challenged man's personal chef?"

"How much does the position pay," Victoria comically asked.

Any prior guard that Victoria had built around herself or had designs on building were dismissed.

Victoria listened as Thomas revealed more about his past life. Although he had never taken the time to learn the language, French always intrigued him. Thomas spoke about past romantic experiences during his college years which for one reason or another never got off the ground. Again, he touched on his love of jazz and mentioned several clubs he used to frequent while in Europe, where jazz continued to reign supreme.

The conversation continued to flow back and forth with ease. They both realized that it was a matter of compatibility—or in another view of the situation it was all about probability and outcome. Either way, Victoria considered it a win-win for her and she felt blessed.

Jasmine had been put to bed hours earlier. Victoria and Thomas talked until well past nine o'clock, before he realized it may be time for him to leave. Victoria tried to convince him otherwise.

"I'd better get going before I run out of things to talk about," Thomas said.

"Ditto on the conversation. I might have to break out in a song and dance to keep you from falling asleep," Victoria jokingly threatened.

"I play a mean piano," Thomas offered.

"Lunch tomorrow?" Thomas asked. "Twelve-thirty."

Victoria lay in bed thinking about her evening with Thomas. Victoria was unsure how an office romance would affect her career or if it was something either one of them should pursue. The phrase friends and lovers could just as easily evolve into oil and vinegar if not handled properly. However, Victoria decided that she was going to take full advantage of whatever happened between her and Thomas. It didn't matter what people who were on the sidelines had to say because this was her life and the choices were hers alone.

It had been months since Gayle attended church on any day of the week other than a Sunday. On Wednesday nights the Deacons and Elders held prayer and financial collection services for the sick and shut in. However, Gayle's motivation for attending in the middle of the week was strictly personal. Taking care of Wesley on a day-to-day basis was certainly no walk in the park. Over the past several weeks he had become increasingly distant, almost to the point of being depressed. More often than not he became increasingly argumentative .

There were times when he would lose focus and she had to remind him who or what they were talking about.

Gayle recalled a recent conversation they had about having someone come in and repair the dishwasher. When she mentioned having her brother take a look at it, Wesley had no idea who she was speaking of much less acknowledging that she had a brother. Making matters worse, it was only last summer that Steven and his wife spent two weeks with them. Gayle wondered how much time would pass before Wesley lost the ability to recognize her as his companion and wife.

After church services earlier in the day, Gayle took the opportunity to speak with Pastor Hinsdale in an effort to uplift her from a spiritual point of view. She also spoke about the state of her marriage. It wasn't easy talking about Wesley behind his back, but this was something Gayle had to do.

"Gayle, you have to remember that God loves you and Wesley no matter what. You're the last person on earth that I have to remind about the power of faith and the changes it can bring about even in the most difficult of times."

As the pastor spoke Gayle instinctively pulled her bible closer to her chest remembering it as the security blanket she relied upon.

"The Lord God has a plan for each and every one of his children and just when the road in life appears unbearable that's when He's there to lift you up." The pastor's hand rested on Gayle's right shoulder while he spoke. He wanted to make Gayle understand that although he was simply God's messenger, she should take his words to heart.

"This is not a matter of losing faith pastor, it's more than that. The plain truth is that sometimes I don't feel physically up to the challenge. Don't get me wrong, I love Wesley as much as any woman can love a man but sometimes . . ."

Gayle hesitated for a moment. The last thing she wanted to do was to say the wrong thing or have her words misinterpreted, even by a man of God.

As the last few members of the congregation filed out of the church, Gayle lowered her tone. There was no need for anyone else to hear their conversation.

"At times I feel the only way Wesley will have a complete and productive life would be to put his care in the hands of a professional. From the literature I've read there are places and services available for that kind of thing. But at the same time, I'm not sure I can go through with what seems like abandoning a loved one," Gayle revealed.

The pastor looked at Gayle and noticed a high level of vacillation, stress and pain on her face.

"Have you spoken with Victoria about this?" he asked.

"I can't discuss something like this with her," Gayle responded as tears began to spill over the cup of her eyes. She tried to pull them back but failed and resigned to let them spill forth.

"It's hard enough even thinking about having to make that kind of decision on my own. Bringing something like this to Victoria would be heartbreaking to say the least," Gayle sorrowfully said.

"I see what you mean. But you can't keep this from her that would be a huge mistake. You have to remember that you're talking about her father. Perhaps you can convince Victoria to stop by this week and we can talk," the pastor suggested.

"I'll do my best, but I can't make any promises," Gayle said. In spite of her faith and the pastor's words Gayle was not sure exactly how to approach Victoria or to convince her to have a conversation with a spiritual advisor.

Again, Gayle tugged at her bible.

"May the Lord bless and keep you," were the pastor's final words.

Wesley was sitting on the couch in the living room which by Gayle's definition was his favorite place in the house outside of the bed. His were eyes trained on a photo album in his lap. He looked at each page before moving on to the next. Wesley recognized some of the photos before him. But with others, his face twisted back and forth as if the answers were on the tip of his tongue, yet the connection with his brain could not be made.

When he heard Gayle enter the room Wesley slammed the album shut as if hiding a secret.

"My goodness, I haven't seen that photo album in years. What made you bring that thing out of the archives?" Gayle asked as she approached.

"I was in the den looking for my gardening journals and there it was on the shelf," Wesley sheepishly responded.

Gayle took a seat next to Wesley and picked up the photo album from his lap. Gayle turned past several pages then stopped when she reached a photo of her brother and his wife at a family gathering about five years ago. They were celebrating their tenth anniversary. Gayle recalled how happy she was when they finally set a wedding date after almost a full year of being engaged. During that period Wesley constantly joked how Gayle's brother was afraid of having to walk down the aisle for the first time.

It was then that Gayle felt as if a cold hand had slapped her across the face leaving her bruised and battered.

Wesley had asked about the images and the people in the photograph. Their names and what the celebration involved.

"You know who that is, stop kidding around. That's my brother and his wife Shirley." Gayle hoped that the leading tone in her voice would help refresh Wesley's mind. She watched closely as he tried to recall memories or interactions he had with the people in the photograph.

Wesley scratched the left side of his head before offering a response.

"Are you sure I know these people?" he asked in a tone that appeared to challenge Gayle's words.

Gayle noticed how Wesley's frustration level rose each time he attempted to recall certain events in his life. It was always the same leaving Gayle concerned about what may happen next. Her heart began to beat faster.

Without notice Wesley took the album from Gayle and in an unprovoked fit of rage, threw the album across the room. It made contact with one of the ceramic vases on the bookshelf. A wedding gift that he himself loved.

Gayle was frozen with a sense of fear and self-preservation. It had been a while since Wesley had displayed any violent tendencies. She believed that phase of his disease was under control when considering the fact that she made sure he kept up with his regiment of medications.

Yet as evidenced by the current situation, there were no guarantees.

Wesley rose to his feet with his hands clinched at his side.

"You're telling me that I should know the people in that damn book of yours, well I don't," Wesley declared.

Although there was a measure of defiance in Wesley's voice, Gayle also noticed a sense of fear finding its way through his emotional outburst.

"Calm down Wesley," Gayle hurriedly said. By this time Wesley had moved toward the door leading to the basement. His right hand rested on the doorknob. Gayle wasn't sure if she should approach him and run the risk of once again being verbally assaulted. Just as important, Gayle worried about Wesley's health. Specifically, his heart. Wesley had undergone bypass surgery to clear two blocked arteries that were severely clogged. He cheated and escaped a serious condition once before and if he didn't calm down right now things may get progressively worse.

"You need to think about your health. Remember what happened the last time you lost control of your emotions, you wound up in the hospital," Gayle warned.

"What are you talking about?" Wesley responded now facing Gayle.

It was hard for Gayle to believe that Wesley failed to remember what had happened to him and how the entire family had been affected. It would seem that anyone would recall being hospitalized. Gayle reminded Wesley of the facts related to his stay.

After Gayle had finished speaking there was no sign that Wesley accepted her words as being the truth.

"I can't take any more of this. I'm going out," Wesley threatened.

"Where are you going?" The last thing Gayle wanted was to let Wesley out of her sight. There was no telling what may happen. The important thing to do right now was to try and remain as calm as possible. Gayle realized that if she portrayed signs of losing control the situation could spiral out of bounds in no time at all.

Something had to be done to reach Wesley and pull him back from the edge toward a place of mental wellness. Gayle was tempted to call the doctor to seek out another person's advice. But she decided it was time that she handled things on her own. Yes, Wesley had given her a scare but she had to learn to live with his episodes until a decision demanded her full attention regarding his long-term care.

Instead of walking over to the front door when threatening to leave, Wesley stopped in his tracks. Gayle could see what appeared to be an out of body experience creep over him. Wesley froze in his tracks as if he were lost in the woods being undecided which way to turn toward safety. However, seconds later, everything appeared to be as clear as a proverbial bell. The color returned to Wesley's face and his eyes focused on the world around him once again.

Wesley made a full body turn in Gayle's direction before he spoke.

"How was church services today?" Wesley asked.

The question in its clarity momentarily shook Gayle to her core. She could hardly believe the change in Wesley's overall status.

"The pastor gave a beautiful sermon this morning, straight from the book of Proverbs. The Lord's spirit filled every nook and cranny of the church," Gayle said.

"You missed a good one," she added.

"I hope you covered for my absence," Wesley said.

"I did the best that I could," Gayle said.

Wesley exploded with one of his famous belly laughs, shaking his head as he climbed the stairs.

As far as Gayle was concerned her world continued to spin on an axis of confusion. Gayle wondered how much longer she could continue to ride the roller coaster that her husband's mind delivered. As suggested, there was no choice and she had to speak with Victoria about the possibility of finding a suitable place with regard to her father. At this line move one space down. There was no getting around it.

Victoria returned to her office after the staff meeting had ended mentally locked in a deficiency of focus. The meeting was as uninformative and just as draining on her body. Its message may as well have been delivered in Latin or some other language which Victoria could not understand.

The truth be told, it was not the subject that left Victoria mentally detached, it was her mother's decision to place dad in an assisted living home. They talked about it, fought about it and afterward stopped speaking to one another for days. This was her father and Victoria believed that she should been made part of the final decision and not just the discussion. In a word Victoria felt cheated.

Sure, mom had to live with dad on a day-to-day basis and maybe suffer through his verbal attacks, but that was no reason to put him out. Victoria failed to understand the one-sided decision and how dad must have felt. Did he understand what was happening? Did he have the mental capacity to appreciate mom's position?

Lost within her thoughts, Victoria was completely unaware of the knock on her door. Getting no response, Rachel decided to enter when Victoria finally recognized her presence.

"Are you alright?" Rachel asked.

"What?" Victoria responded as if the question was not applicable to her current status.

"I've only been standing here for ten minutes," Rachel said in mock frustration.

"Really, ten minutes?" Victoria asked.

"Well not exactly ten minutes, but a really long time," Rachel said. "Are you okay, you seemed out of it for a while there."

“And then some,” Victoria said sounding more exhausted than she actually felt.

“Want to talk about it?” Rachel asked obviously concerned about her friend.

“Not really. What’s up?” Victoria asked.

“I have that color layout you wanted to review,” Rachel said.

“Okay, thanks.” Although Victoria really appreciated Rachel’s efforts, it didn’t come through in her response.

Rachel noticed.

“Are you sure everything’s fine?” Rachel pressed.

“I’m okay, really. I have to talk to my mother about something,” Victoria replied without much enthusiasm.

“All right. But remember if you need a sympathetic ear, I’m there for you and my rates are extremely reasonable,” Rachel said smiling as she left.

Victoria realized that there had to be a meeting of the mind as far as dad was concerned. The sad part of it all was the fact that Jasmine heard the argument she and mom had on the phone the other day. It was extremely heated and they said things to each other that were not meant for anyone else to hear; especially a young child.

Victoria came to realize the only option left was to speak with mom face to face and maybe even apologize. Whatever pride Victoria held onto had to be discharged. She had to look at things from her mother’s perspective. Victoria needed to realize how hard it must have been for mom to place dad’s care in the hands of strangers. Something awful must have happened that she didn’t know about that backed mom into a corner.

“Grandma, are we going to see grandpa today?” Jasmine asked from the back seat of the car. There was a sense of excitement in her voice as if she had not seen the man in years. It was grandfather’s day and Jasmine made Wesley a special gift that she couldn’t wait to give to him.

“You’ll have to ask your mother,” Gayle responded.

“Of course we are,” Victoria responded over her shoulder and in Jasmine’ direction.

Over the past two weeks mother and daughter had covered so much territory when it came to the family and everything it meant. Victoria finally realized how much mom had suffered because of dad. Unintentional of course, but Victoria was amazed to find out how strong her mother had been when it came to dealing with dad's illness. Victoria never realized how much her mother had to give up in caring for dad. So much of what mom had to endure remained trapped within the walls of their house as secrets yet to be revealed. Sadly, it reached a point where mom could not adequately service dad's needs.

Wesley refused to eat the meals that she prepared, believing that she was only there to harm him. There were nights that dad refused to sleep in the same bed with mom. This bothered her more than his verbal attacks. Although Gayle knew that prayer and her faith in the Lord meant everything, things had come to a point where she had to take matters into her own hands and face the facts that lay in front of her.

Although mom had forgiven her, Victoria could not shake the guilt and shame which coursed through her body. The phrase about time healing all wounds were never more appropriate than the here and now.

Gayle, Victoria and Jasmine entered the lobby of the Glenn R. Morning View assisted living facility. Jasmine was obviously filled with questions about this being her grandfather's new home. Victoria tried her best to answer in a way that Jasmine could understand.

As the trio approached the receptionist's area they were greeted by a member of the staff. The man appeared to waddle from side to side as he walked. Although Gayle and Victoria had been to the facility on prior occasions, this was their first encounter with this particular staff member.

"Mrs. Grant, Ms. Reynolds I'm very pleased to meet you. I'm Dr. Tylerman and I've been assigned to supervise Mr. Grant's care."

Turning his attention to Jasmine.

"And who do we have here?" Tylerman cheerfully asked as he bent forward almost in a full bow.

Jasmine looked toward her mother and grandmother before responding and giving her name.

Turning to Victoria, Tylerman asked if she would like Jasmine to play in their children's section while they spoke in private.

"There are all sorts of video games, internet access, hundreds of books and puzzles." Tylerman made it sound like every child's fantasy come true.

"Wouldn't you rather pay grandpa a visit first?"

Moments later, the doctor led Gayle and Victoria down a brightly lit hallway and around the corner from where they initially met. His office was three doors down from the exit sign.

"As I said before I was only recently assigned to Mr. Grant's case, but from what I've seen thus far things have been going rather well. There have been minimal outbreaks with the staff and for the most part Mr. Grant been a model resident."

Tylerman turned toward Gayle.

"That being said, there have been bouts of difficulty in getting your husband to take his medicine and exercise more than twice a day. But we're working on that and expect things to change in a relatively short period of time."

There was a look on compassion and confidence on the doctor's face which had not gone unnoticed by Gayle or her daughter.

Tylerman flipped through a chart on his desk before continuing to speak. He also waited in the event that either Victoria or her mother had any questions or comments to make.

"You seemed to have arrived just before lunch and Mr. Grant's medication time. If you like I can schedule a brief sit down before then?"

"Perfect," Gayle responded.

Victoria nodded in agreement.

Tylerman placed a phone call to the front desk to lock down the visit.

"Yes, three visitors. They have been properly screened." He flashed the thumbs up sign to Gayle and Victoria as he spoke.

Okay, now that that's settled, do you know your way to the community room on the third floor?"

"Yes we do," Victoria immediately responded."

"Dr. Florentine took us there when he gave us a tour of the facility on our first visit."

As Gayle and Victoria entered the community room, the smell of liquid pine hit their nostrils, followed by the scent of menthol infused joint pain cream. There were men standing near one of the three gated windows looking toward the sky above. They were making jabbing motions and muttering to one another in a language that appeared to be English, but it was terribly unrecognizable. To their left were two elderly men seated at a folding table engaged in a game of checkers. However, after several moments of watching them, Victoria noticed that neither man made an effort to move their respective pieces around the board. It appeared as if one were waiting on the other to decide who should move next.

Although the television blared loudly no one seemed to be paying much attention to what was being said. They failed to stop and acknowledge the lead story which told of a robbery that had taken place last evening on Sullivan Avenue, only two blocks away.

Moments later a staff worker appeared.

"You must be here to see Mr. Grant. Hello I'm Jimmy, James Wright if you want formality. I take care most of the residents on this ward. Ask anyone. I do a great job with these guys too," he bragged without any solicitation.

It appeared to Victoria that the young man was seeking their approval for doing his job.

"That's fine," Gayle responded. "Yes, we're here to see Mr. Grant. I'm his wife and this is his daughter Victoria," Gayle said.

"Oh yeah, they called from downstairs and said that we should be expecting you. He'll be here in just a minute."

A short time later Wesley was being wheeled into the room by a young female staffer. Wesley's arms were crossed over his chest and he stared straight ahead without much of an expression on his face. He was wearing the Blue and yellow jogging suit Gayle bought for his birthday last year and a pair of white sneakers. The woman stopped in front of the only unoccupied table in the room and left Wesley there without saying a word. There were a few magazines on the table but it was clear that he was not interested.

The woman signaled to Jimmy that it was okay for the resident's guests to come over and begin their visit.

The entire scene left a sour taste in Victoria's mouth, but she chose not to focus on the negative.

Gayle sat down to his right and Victoria took the seat directly across.

"Wesley it's me," Gayle said as she lifted her husband's right hand from his lap. Her voice was gentle and soft.

At the sound of the female voice Wesley's mind sprang to life and a sudden glow of recognition appeared on his face. It was almost as if he'd run into a long-lost friend after so many years of being apart.

"Gayle, oh my God it's so good to see you. I've missed you so much," Wesley said. The sound of his voice seemed to fill the entire room.

Other residents trained their attention on the sound. Some with a look of disapproval.

Victoria wondered how much of dad's greeting was genuine and truly meant for the woman who had stood by her father or was this some random and spontaneous reaction to seeing anyone in his field of vision.

However, Victoria's questions and doubts were answered.

"Vicky it's about time you got here." His hands reached out to his daughter and the pair embraced for several seconds.

Wesley turned his attention to Jasmine who was standing at her mother's side.

"Jasmine," Wesley said in a sing song type of voice.

Jasmine leapt into her grandfather's lap knocking the unlocked wheelchair back a few inches.

"Oh my lord look at you," Wesley said.

"You must have grown a full two feet since I last saw you. Vicky what have you been feeding my grandchild," he asked through a wide smile etched his face.

From her view Victoria could see that dad appeared to be in good shape, although it looked as if he'd lost a few pounds and hadn't shaved in a day or two.

But once again, the current surroundings caused Victoria to think about the man her dad used to be. There were days when it seemed that nothing would bother him and he could do everything. Yet Victoria realized that as time had changed and as she watched her parents interact, she would have to show her love to dad in a different way. Nothing less, just differently.

Gayle, Victoria and Jasmine listened to Wesley's stories covering the past few weeks. His complaints touched on the menu, the fact that he had to be in bed at a certain time and he was forced to exercise when he didn't feel like it. At times Wesley's descriptions of the events were down right hilarious and at other times his renditions pulled at the heart. But more importantly, Victoria could see that dad was absolutely clear in his thought process. There were no signs of frustration or an inability to recall past events. For some reason dad weaved in an accident Victoria had as a child where she fell down and skinned her knees.

Wesley lowered his voice slightly as he rolled out his next story involving one of the guests. This was how he referred to everyone outside of the staff.

"There's this guy that sleeps in the room next to mine, I think his name is Lester. The man snores loud enough to turn a block of wood in to sawdust at the drop of a hat. Everyone around here calls him Buzz because of it. The man is like a human chainsaw." As Wesley spoke, he laughed and secretly pointed to a man standing next to the water dispenser in the far-right corner of the room. Wesley then spoke about the death of a woman on his floor named Ethel Reese. For Gayle, it was strange hearing her husband speak so fondly about the woman as if he had known her for a large part of his life, when in reality that was not the case.

Victoria could have sworn that she saw a tear in her father's eyes as he revealed how Ethel was found in her room after dinner last week. She apparently passed comfortably in her sleep.

"She was a wonderful person," Wesley said with a tone filled with sadness.

Wesley sat quietly leaving Gayle and Victoria to wonder what memories he may have of this woman that they were not privy too. Somewhere in his world there appeared to be an emotional attachment. Considering the way he spoke about her and the look on his face, Gayle felt there was a possibility, but she immediately dismissed the thought as her being ridiculous.

"You haven't been giving the staff any problems about taking your medication have you?" Gayle asked sharply and lovingly at the same time.

There was no response.

"Wesley," Gayle said with emphasis and a nudge of his arm.

Victoria and Jasmine could not hold back the smile that appeared on their faces.

"Uh oh grandpa," Jasmine said. "You're in trouble now, she added.

"Well," Wesley began sheepishly. "By the time I get out of here I'm going to be the healthiest pin cushion ever. It seems if I'm not being poked and ordered to swallow one pill or another, the sun won't come out tomorrow morning."

Epilogue

One year later—Channingston, Long Island New York.

"Mom, Thomas said that he would take me shopping at the mall on Saturday if I passed my math test," Jasmine said with a sparkle of anticipation registered across her face.

"That doesn't sound like something he would promise. Especially when it came to school work, he's very serious about that kind of thing you know," Victoria said.

"He did. You can ask him when he comes downstairs," Jasmine replied with conviction.

"I'll make a deal with you. Finish putting your things away, clean your room and you'll get something from me on Saturday as well," Victoria said.

"Hey that's bribery," Jasmine countered.

"No. That's called a parents prerogative and someday you'll get to use it on your own child," Victoria replied attempting to maintain a serious look on her face.

Jasmine thought long and hard about her mother's response before turning her thoughts to other matters.

"Maybe we can take a drive and visit grandma and grandpa?" Jasmine suggested.

"We'll see. But let's not bite off more than we can chew. The math test comes first. Now hurry up and get moving," Victoria urged.

"I heard every word of that," Thomas said as he approached Victoria from behind.

"That so?" Victoria replied as she turned toward her husband.

"Rumor has it that young lady has you wrapped around her little fingers," Victoria charged.

"That may be true, but rumor also has it that I have this lady wrapped around my finger," Thomas replied as he pulled Victoria closer to him.

Thomas and Victoria embraced and deeply kissed. One holding the other in a romantic embrace for several moments.

"Are you serious about taking Jasmine to see your dad this weekend?" Thomas asked.

"I think so, but I haven't decided yet. The best I can do right now is talk to mom and see how she's getting along. She went to see him last week on her own so . . ." Victoria intentionally choked off the rest of her sentence.

"I have to hand it to her. Your mother seems to have bounced back in spite of everything that has happened," Thomas said in a complimentary manner.

"True. She's some special kind of person. But if I've told you once, I've told you a thousand times—you're surrounded by three remarkable women and don't you ever forget it," Victoria playfully remarked.

"Okay, but when the baby arrives, our son that is, at least I'll have a fighting chance," Thomas boastfully responded.

"Wanna bet?" Victoria responded.

-The End-

www.ingramcontent.com/pod-product-compliance
Lightning Source LLC
Chambersburg PA
CBHW030145010826
48973CB00002B/738

* 9 7 8 1 9 6 3 0 6 8 3 3 7 *